Molly's br
seen a sun

"And I have never seen anything like you framed by the sunset," he said.

Then his mouth covered hers.

His lips were warm and firm, confident in their mastery. And, once again, there was no hesitation in her response.

The warm strength of his arms around her wasn't just familiar, it was right. And the explosion of sensations made her mind spin, her heart pound and her body yearn.

He found the pins that held her twist in place and slipped them out so that her hair spilled into his hands. His fingers sifted through the tresses, caught the ends to tip her head back, changing the angle and deepening the kiss.

She wanted him—there was no denying that fact. But she couldn't let herself get caught up in the moment, the romance, the fantasy.

There was too much at stake now.

Dear Reader,

The holidays have always been my favorite time of the year, but there's one thing that makes every season even better—a touch of romance.

Prince Eric Santiago isn't looking for any long-term involvements when he meets a sexy bartender on a visit to Texas; Molly Shea never expected one night with a stranger to alter the course of her life. But everything changes for both of them when they learn that she's expecting a royal baby!

He's a man who wants to do the right thing; she's a woman who refuses to marry except for love. Throw them together on an island paradise and they just might realize their goals aren't so different after all. And maybe there will be wedding bells in Tesoro del Mar this December....

Happy Holidays!

Brenda Harlen

THE PRINCE'S HOLIDAY BABY

BRENDA HARLEN

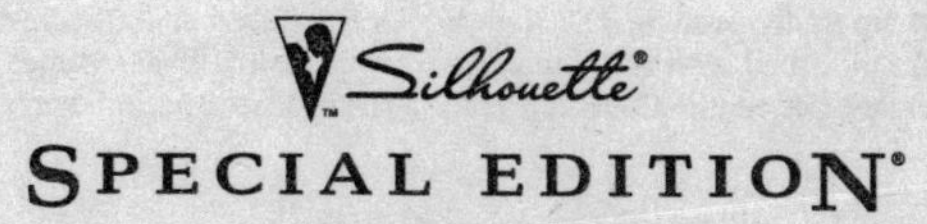

Published by Silhouette Books
America's Publisher of Contemporary Romance

Recycling programs for this product may not exist in your area.

ISBN-13: 978-0-373-24942-8
ISBN-10: 0-373-24942-X

THE PRINCE'S HOLIDAY BABY

This edition published by arrangement with Harlequin Books S.A.

Visit Silhouette Books at www.eHarlequin.com

Printed in U.S.A.

Books by Brenda Harlen

Silhouette Special Edition

Once and Again #1714
**Her Best-Kept Secret* #1756
The Marriage Solution #1811
†*One Man's Family* #1827
The New Girl in Town #1859
***The Prince's Royal Dilemma* #1898
***The Prince's Cowgirl Bride* #1920
††*Family in Progress* #1928
***The Prince's Holiday Baby* #1942

Silhouette Romantic Suspense

McIver's Mission #1224
Some Kind of Hero #1246
Extreme Measures #1282
Bulletproof Hearts #1313
Dangerous Passions #1394

*Family Business
†Logan's Legacy Revisited
**Reigning Men
††Back in Business

BRENDA HARLEN

grew up in a small town surrounded by books and imaginary friends. Although she always dreamed of being a writer, she chose to follow a more traditional career path first. After two years of practicing as an attorney (including an appearance in front of the Supreme Court of Canada), she gave up her "real" job to be a mom and to try her hand at writing books. Three years, five manuscripts and another baby later, she sold her first book—an RWA Golden Heart Winner—to Silhouette Books.

Brenda lives in southern Ontario with her real-life husband/hero, two heroes-in-training and two neurotic dogs. She is still surrounded by books ("too many books," according to her children) and imaginary friends, but she also enjoys communicating with "real" people. Readers can contact Brenda by e-mail at brendaharlen@yahoo.com or by snail mail c/o Silhouette Books, 233 Broadway, Suite 1001, New York, NY 10279.

In memory of Tom Torrance—
January 28, 1951–March 6, 2008

A teacher and mentor and friend;
a genuine prince among men.

Prologue

"You didn't need to come over here, Grandma. I told you on the phone that I was fine."

Theresa Shea plunked her purse on the bar and narrowed her gaze on her granddaughter behind the counter at Shea's Bar & Grill. Yes, she certainly looked fine. But Molly had always been one to keep her chin up no matter how much her heart was breaking inside. And she'd had a lot of heartbreak to deal with over the past six months.

"Maybe I needed to see for myself."

"And now you have."

"And now that I'm here, maybe I'd like a cup of coffee."

Molly poured her a cup of coffee, pushed it across the counter.

She'd been working there for so many years now, she didn't even have to think about the tasks anymore. Everything was automatic, routine, and not at all what James Shea wanted for his daughter.

"What are you doing here?" Theresa asked softly.

"Right now? Trying to figure out the produce order for next week."

"He wanted you to go to college, to do something more."

Her granddaughter's fingers tightened around the pencil in her hand, but there was no other outward sign of the emotions that were churning inside her. Molly didn't talk about her father but Theresa knew he was in her thoughts almost constantly, especially here, at the restaurant that had been his livelihood and his life. And she knew that Molly was so determined to hold on to Shea's because it was the only part of her father she had left.

"I'm happy here," Molly finally said.

"Are you?"

Molly continued punching numbers into the calculator, frowned.

Theresa tried a different tack. "Do you ever write anymore?"

"I write checks to pay the bills."

"You know that's not what I meant."

"It's all I have time for right now."

"You have to learn to take time for the things that are more enoyable than necessary."

"I will," Molly promised. "After all the necessary things are done."

Theresa picked up her purse. She knew when she was banging her head against a wall and her granddaughter's stubbornness was a brick wall.

"All right, I'll go. But if you need anything—"

Molly leaned across the counter to kiss her grandmother's cheek. "I won't. I'll be fine."

Which was exactly why Theresa was worried.

The phone rang as she turned away, and Molly reached for it. Theresa didn't hear the words she spoke, but the tone gave her pause. When Molly hung up, she said only one word, "Abbey."

Molly's sister, Theresa's youngest granddaughter, had disappeared a few days earlier after leaving a note that said only "don't worry—I'll be home in a few days" and absolutely nothing about where she was going or who she was with.

"Where is she?"

"Las Vegas." Molly swallowed. "With Jason."

Theresa didn't want to ask, was certain she already knew, and her granddaughter's next words confirmed it.

"She just married my fiancé."

Chapter One

Nine years later—

Prince Eric Santiago lied when he told his best friend that he had a plane to catch. The truth was, his pilot wasn't coming to pick him up for the return trip to Tesoro del Mar until the following morning, but after almost two weeks with Scott Delsey and his soon-to-be-wife, Eric needed some space. Spending so much time with the blissful couple and seeing how in love they were only made him more aware of what was missing from his own life.

When he'd accepted the invitation to visit Scott's ranch in Texas, he'd thought his friend might want to offer him a job at DELconnex, his communications company. On more than one occasion in the past, Scott had mentioned that he could use someone with Eric's education and experience, though they both knew Eric had no intention of leaving the Tesorian navy.

Now, of course, the situation had changed, and Eric was willing to consider any possibilities his friend presented. It turned out one of those possibilities was to stand up as the best man at Scott's wedding.

It seemed that everywhere around him people were getting married and having babies. First it was his eldest brother, Rowan, who had been forced by tragedy and tradition to the altar. Luckily for him, he'd managed to fall in love along the way. After six years of marriage, he and Lara were happier than the day they'd exchanged their vows, even with—or maybe because of—the two active young sons who did their best to run their parents ragged.

Three years after Rowan pledged "till death do us part," their youngest brother, Marcus, had found a woman who inspired him to do the same. Recently, he and Jewel had welcomed their first child into the world—a beautiful baby girl who looked just like her mother and already exhibited the legendary charm of her father.

Both of his brothers had lucked out, and Eric was genuinely happy for them. But the only mistress Eric had ever been committed to was the sea—and she'd tossed him aside, carelessly discarding everything he'd given her and taking away everything he was.

As he drove his rented Mercedes northeast toward San Antonio, he forced himself to acknowledge the truth he'd been avoiding for too long—he wasn't just alone, he was lonely.

He envied what Rowan had with Lara, what Marcus had with Jewel, what Scott had with Fiona. And he wondered why he'd never met a woman who made him think in terms of marriage and forever. Okay, having spent the better part of the last twelve years on board a ship might have something to do with it. Add to that the uncertainty of never knowing if the women he'd been with were genuinely interested in him or only attracted to his title or his uniform, and it probably wasn't surprising that he'd reached the age of thirty-six without ever having been in a long-term, committed relationship. Still, the realization wasn't going to fill his life or keep him warm in bed at night.

The rumble of his stomach finally broke through his introspection and a neon sign announcing Shea's Bar & Grill snagged his attention.

Despite the fact that the building was smack in the middle of nowhere, there were several vehicles—mostly dust-covered pickup trucks—in the parking lot. His empty stomach again protested his decision to leave his friend's ranch before dinner and he flicked on his indicator to make the turn.

He parked his shiny rental between an ancient red pickup and a mud-splattered Jeep and sat for a moment, wondering if he would look as out of place in the bar as his vehicle did in the parking lot. A man who'd grown up in the public eye wouldn't usually worry about such things, but Eric had become more sensitive to the attention—and the speculation that surrounded him—since the accident.

He pushed out of the car, slowly limped toward the entrance. The deliberate, unhurried movements helped ease the stiffness from his hip so that he was walking almost normally by the time he reached the door. His therapist had warned that he might always have the limp and the discomfort—at the time, he'd thought it was a small price to pay for being alive. When he'd had to leave the navy, he'd realized the physical scars weren't the biggest price.

A sign inside the door invited him to seat himself. He bypassed several empty tables around the perimeter of the dance floor and made his way to the bar. As he slid onto a vacant stool, he forgot about his hip and everything else as he glimpsed a vision that was more impressive than anything he'd seen while sightseeing in Texas.

Hermoso...espectacular...perfecto.

Her hair was as dark as midnight and tumbled over her shoulders like a silky waterfall. She was wearing a deep, V-neck shirt that revealed just a hint of cleavage and was tucked into slim-fitting jeans that molded to narrow hips and long legs.

His gaze skimmed upward again and locked with hers.

He felt a sharp tug of attraction deep in his belly, an almost painful yearning, and he could tell by the sudden widening and darkening of eyes the color of a clear summer sky that she was experiencing the same sensation. Instantaneous, raw and powerful.

But then she tossed her hair over her shoulder and smiled easily.

"Hey, handsome." The slow Texas drawl made him think of lazy Sunday mornings spent lounging in bed—and wasn't *that* an unexpectedly intriguing image? "What can I get for you?"

She smiled again, and suddenly he was wanting a lot more than he'd come in for, but he forced himself to respond just as casually. "A beer would be good."

She grabbed a clean mug from the shelf behind her. "Any particular kind?"

He tore his gaze from the stunning face to glance at the labels on the taps. He noted the familiar Amstel, Heineken and Beck's brands, but opted for one that he guessed would have a more local flavor. "Lone Star."

She tipped the glass beneath the nozzle to catch the amber-colored liquid that flowed out. "You're a long way from home, aren't you?"

"Am I?"

She slid the beer across the bar to him. "Well, you don't sound like a local, and if you were, I would have seen you before now."

He didn't think she was flirting with him exactly. But she seemed, if not interested, at least curious, and he couldn't resist testing the waters.

"You don't remember?" he asked, his tone intended to convey both disbelief and disappointment.

She made change for the ten he gave her and leaned across the bar in a way that greatly enhanced his view of her cleavage. "If I don't remember, *you* obviously didn't make much of an impression."

He grinned at her quick response and lifted his glass to his lips as she moved down the bar to serve another customer.

He'd struck out with the sexy bartender, but it was his first time at bat after a long absence from the plate and, the way he figured it, it was only the top of the first inning. There was a lot of the game still to be played.

Eric ordered a barbecued pork sandwich with a side of spicy fries and washed it down with another draft as he watched the woman who'd eventually introduced herself as Molly Shea check on her customers at the bar. She took a moment to chat with each one as if they were all old friends, and he knew some of them probably were.

"How long have you been a bartender?" he asked her.

She poured a glass of water and squeezed a wedge of lime into it. "Forever."

"Has it always been your ambition?"

"It's honest work," she said.

"I wasn't implying otherwise," he told her. "You just seem like a woman who could do so much more."

"I can make all the fanciest drinks," she said, deliberately misunderstanding him. "But we don't have much call for them here."

"You're determined not to give away anything about yourself, aren't you?"

"Bartenders don't make confessions, they listen to them."

"I thought that was just a stereotype."

"I used to think so, too. But I learned quickly that a sympathetic ear and a shot of Scotch whiskey is a lot more successful at loosening tongues than a long couch and a fifty-minute clock."

His gaze skimmed over her face. "The ears are nice," he agreed. "But I'll bet it has a lot more to do with your soft voice and warm smile." And the idea of this woman on a long couch—minus the fifty-minute clock—was more than a little intriguing.

"Is that why you're here?" she asked. "Are you looking to unburden your soul?"

"My soul isn't burdened."

Her only response was to raise her eyebrows.

"No more than most," he clarified.

She smiled at that, and he felt a funny little kick in his belly. It was lust, he was certain of it. Certain that what he was feeling for this intriguing bartender couldn't be any more than that.

Eric picked up his cup and frowned when he found it empty. He'd switched to coffee after his second draft, and he'd already had one refill, making him wonder just how long he'd been sitting at the bar.

"It's almost eleven," Molly told him, somehow anticipating his question as she brought the pot over to refill his cup again. "Isn't there somewhere else you should be?"

"Not anymore," he told her.

Her eyes were unexpectedly sympathetic as she asked, "Did she kick you out?"

"Who?"

"Whoever's responsible for that lost look in your eyes."

"No one kicked me out." Then he smiled at her. "Not yet, anyway."

She laughed. "You've got another hour."

* * *

He was still there at the end of the hour.

And Molly was still as conscious of his presence as she'd been from the minute he walked in the door. Conscious of his attention focused on her as she began tidying up her workspace and wiping down the counters after last call.

She was flattered, of course. The man was sinfully good looking with that dark hair and those smoldering eyes, a mouth that made her think of long, slow kisses and shoulders that looked as if they could carry the weight of the world.

But he didn't belong there. She'd recognized that fact even before he'd opened his mouth and started speaking in that smoothly cultured voice that spoke of private schools and a wealth of other privileges.

And she wondered what he was doing in Texas or, more particularly, what he was doing in her bar.

She did know that every time she caught him looking at her, her pulse spiked. And when he smiled, her heart pounded and her blood heated. Though her experience with men was limited, she recognized her reaction for what it was: lust, pure and simple. And when a man looked like the one sitting at her bar, she was certain he had more than enough experience being the object of women's desires.

The stirring of her own desire, however, was unexpected.

She wasn't the type of woman to fantasize about having sex with a man she didn't even know. Of course, her lackluster experience with Trevor had pretty much nixed her fantasies about sex—and the few brief relationships she'd had since then hadn't given her reason to hope for anything different.

But she poured herself a single glass of wine—part of her usual closing up routine—and slid onto the stool beside his. "Are you really waiting for me to kick you out?"

"I'm not in a hurry to go anywhere else."

"If I'm going to let you stay while I close up, I'll need to know more about you."

"Such as?"

"Where you're from—because we both know it's not Texas."

"Tesoro del Mar," he told her.

"Treasure of the Sea," she translated.

"You speak Spanish?"

"A little." She sipped her wine. "And is it—a treasure of the sea, that is?"

"Absolutely."

"What brought you from there to here?"

"I was visiting a friend."

"A girlfriend?" she guessed.

"No," he said, then, "yes, there was a woman."

She lifted a brow. "Only one?"

He smiled. "My best friend is getting married. His fiancée is the only woman I've seen since I've been here."

"How long has that been?"

"Almost two weeks."

"And why is it that you're alone in a bar at quarter after twelve on a Sunday night?"

He made a point of looking her over. "I'm not exactly alone now, am I?"

"Alone *except* for the bartender," she clarified.

"I would say alone *with* an incredibly beautiful woman."

The heat in his gaze added weight to his words, but Molly wasn't going to let herself get all tongue-tied and weak-kneed just because a handsome man paid her a compliment.

"I'm flattered," she said. "But you're going to be disappointed if you think a few smooth words will convince me to go home with you."

"Since I don't even have a hotel room booked, I was hoping

you would invite me to go home with you." There was something in his tone that told her he was only half joking.

"Not going to happen," she told him.

"Is there anyone special in your life?"

She smiled. "There are a lot of special people in my life."

"I meant a boyfriend," he clarified. "Since you're not wearing a ring, I'm guessing there's not a husband or fiancé."

She shook her head. "I don't really have time to date. Too many other things going on."

"That might be a valid excuse for neglecting to return a phone call," he noted, "but it hardly explains not dating."

"Does a broken engagement explain it better for you?"

He nodded. "Broken heart, too?"

She hesitated a moment, then shook her head. "No, and maybe that's one of the reasons I haven't been dating. I realized how close I'd come to making a very big mistake, and I needed some time to figure out what I really wanted."

"And have you?"

"I'm still working on it."

"Me, too," he admitted.

"I would have figured you for the type of man who knew exactly what he wanted."

"I used to be." His eyes held hers for a long moment, then his gaze dropped to her mouth. "Not only did I know what I wanted, but I knew how to get it."

Then he leaned down and kissed her.

And she kissed him back.

She, Molly Shea, who didn't do anything spontaneous or impulsive, was kissing a stranger in a bar—and thoroughly enjoying every second of it.

Because—WOW—he knew how to kiss.

Her brain scrambled to find an explanation for this inexplicable turn of events. She wanted to blame the wine, though she'd only had half a glass. She might consider the lateness of the hour, except that she was accustomed to working nights and wasn't at all tired. Or maybe it was just the strength of a purely physical attraction that she hadn't felt in a very long time.

His tongue slid between her lips and the random thoughts and desperate explanations faded into nothingness as her brain seemed to stop functioning altogether.

His hands slid up her back, drawing her close, closer. Her breasts grazed the solid wall of his chest. Her nipples tightened, her belly quivered. He drew her to her feet, and she pressed herself against him, shocked—and aroused—to feel the hard ridge of his erection against her belly.

He wanted her.

Of course, he was a man and the state of his arousal might have more to do with that fact than the identity of the woman in his arms, but she wasn't going to worry about that now. She was just going to bask in the knowledge that she was wanted, revel in this affirmation of her feminine power. At least for another minute.

Had she ever been kissed so thoroughly? Until her blood felt like molten lava pulsing through her veins and her knees went weak and everything inside her started to quiver? Never.

Not even Trevor's kisses had made her feel like this. He was the first man she'd ever been intimate with, and she'd never responded to him the way she was responding now. Of course, her relationship with Trevor had come on the heels of the break-up of her engagement, when she'd been desperate to feel wanted by someone. But even then, she'd never wanted to be with him as desperately as she wanted to be with Eric now.

And the wanting terrified her.

She forced herself to ease away from him and when she spoke, she kept her voice light, careful to give no hint of the churning inside. "You know what? You're as sexy as sin and when you kiss me, it makes my heart pound like you wouldn't believe, but I don't do one night stands with strangers."

"I don't, either…as a rule." He slid his hands up her back, and she shivered as his fingers traced lazily along the ridges of her spine. "But there's an exception to every rule."

"And you think you should be mine?" she asked skeptically.

"I think *you* could be *mine*."

She pushed his arms down, stepped away from him and temptation. "I might be a small-town girl, but even I can recognize a big-time con."

He winced. "Okay, it did sound like a line."

"You think?" What was even worse than the obvious script was how much she still wanted to give in to the desire thrumming between them.

"What I think is that, for the first time in a long time, I've met an interesting woman and I'm not ready to say goodbye to her yet."

He sounded sincere, but if she'd learned nothing else from her failed relationships, she'd learned that she didn't have a clue when it came to understanding the motivations of men. "Do you mean that?"

"Yes, I do."

His voice was sure, his gaze steady, and despite the doubts and insecurities that swirled inside her, she wasn't ready to say goodbye yet, either.

"I'm not working tomorrow," she finally said. "If you wanted to meet me back here around ten, maybe we could spend the day together."

"I'd really like that," he said. "But I won't be here tomorrow."

Disappointment weighed heavily in her belly. "You won't?"

"My plane's scheduled to leave at 8:00 a.m."

"You're going back to Tesoro del Mar?"

He nodded, and though she regretted that it was true, she knew his leaving wasn't any reason to throw caution to the wind and do something completely crazy.

"I guess this is goodbye then," she said.

"I guess it is," he agreed.

Then he tipped her chin up with his finger and brushed his lips against hers. It was a gentle kiss this time, as fleeting as their time together had been.

"Goodbye, Molly."

"Goodbye." She watched him cross the room. She watched as he flipped the lock and pushed on the door, and she felt all of her reason and common sense sweep through the open portal and into the night.

"Wait." The word sprang from her lips without conscious thought.

He turned back. Waiting.

She could let him go—and always wonder what might have been. Or she could be wildly spontaneous and spend the night with a man whose kiss had singed her right down to her toes.

She'd always believed it was better to regret something she'd done than something she'd left undone, and while it was possible she'd wake up with regrets in the morning, she knew she would regret it more if she let him walk away.

Eric sensed the battle waging inside Molly and it took every ounce of willpower he possessed to keep his hand clamped around the handle of the door to keep from reaching for her again. If they were going to spend the night together—as he very much wanted them to do—it would need to be her decision. And he knew it wasn't one she would make lightly.

She'd admitted that she didn't date much, and he knew a

woman as beautiful and warm and friendly as Molly didn't sleep alone unless it was what she wanted. So what made him think that she would break her self-imposed rules to spend the night with him?

Chemistry.

It had crackled between them from the first moment their eyes had locked across the bar and had been building and deepening ever since. The sizzling kiss they'd shared was further proof of it.

His body was still humming from the after-effects of that kiss, or maybe it was almost three years of self-imposed celibacy that had everything inside him churned up. Whatever the reason, he knew what he wanted. He was just waiting for Molly to reach the same conclusion.

She looked at him now, her eyes locked with his, and she said only one more word.

"Stay."

He flipped the lock on the door and moved back to her.

She met him halfway—her arms lifting to circle his neck, her body pressing against his, her mouth opening for his kiss.

His hands moved over her, hotly, hungrily. She gasped and sighed in response to his touch, and those sexy little sounds nearly snapped the last of his control. She was so eager and passionate, as hungry for him as he was for her, and it was an effort not to tear away her clothes where they stood and bury himself inside her.

The woman had him tied up in knots, desperate and aching with desire.

He cupped her breasts and felt her nipples pebble in response to the brush of his thumbs. She arched against him, a silent plea for more. Even through the layers of their clothing, the erotic friction of her hips pushing against his was almost too much.

She was sexy and sweet, giving and demanding.

And she was his.

The thought came from out of nowhere, the sudden drive to take and claim and possess both unfamiliar and undeniable.

He was leaving in the morning. They both knew they wouldn't have anything more than this one night together. But he was determined to make it a night neither of them would ever forget.

This was crazy.

Even as Molly led Eric up the stairs to her apartment over the bar, she knew it was outrageously insane to even consider having sex with a man she'd never laid eyes on a few hours before, who would be leaving again in another few hours and whom she would probably never see again after that.

She didn't care.

Right now all she cared about was getting naked with him.

And he wanted the same thing, if the trail of clothes they left in the hall on their way to her room was any indication. She led him unerringly through the dark to the bed, then pushed him back onto the mattress and tumbled down with him.

She reached for the small lamp on the night table, but he caught her hand and brought it to his lips. He kissed her palm, nibbled on her fingers, and sent sparks of heat zinging through her system.

Oh, yes, there was heat. And Molly gloried in this confirmation that she wasn't unresponsive or dispassionate, she'd just needed a man who knew how to touch her the right way. And Eric definitely knew how to touch a woman the right way.

She wanted to touch him—was desperate to touch him—too. With limited experience to fall back on, she allowed her instincts to guide her. She ran her hands up his chest, over his shoulders, down his arms. She reveled in the feel of all those hard, tight muscles bunching and flexing in response to her eager touch. His skin was warm and smooth and taut; his body exquisitely carved and sculpted. Everywhere she touched, he was hard and strong, so completely and perfectly male. And for now—for the next few hours that remained of the night—he was hers.

Her fingertips paused in their exploration, hovering over the puckered ridge of skin she'd discovered beneath his lowest rib.

She felt him tense as she slowly traced the diagonal line of the scar toward his hip bone. Her fingers moved lower, finding a wider, longer scar on his upper thigh, and she instinctively knew this was the reason he hadn't wanted the light.

His perfect body wasn't quite perfect after all. And yet, the physical scars on his body somehow enhanced rather than detracted from his appeal.

"A recent injury?" she asked softly.

"Not so recent," he said, but offered nothing more.

She traced her fingertips over the scars again, as if her touch could ease the strain she heard in his voice, the tension in his muscles. "What happened?"

"A naval training exercise went wrong."

His simplistic explanation was a clear indication that this wasn't something he wanted to talk about. But his response had given her another valuable insight about this man. "So you're a sailor."

"Was," he corrected.

"With a woman in every port?" she teased to lighten the moment.

"Never more than one at a time."

"Good to know." She kissed him then, deeply, hungrily.

She kissed his lips, his throat, his chest. Her hair spilled over his shoulders, providing a curtain behind which she continued her exploration. She'd never been so aroused, so tempted, so bold. But she let her instincts, and his throaty groans of appreciation, guide her. She nibbled her way down his belly, savored the salty masculine flavor of his skin. Then her lips found the ridge of scar tissue her fingers had recently discovered, and her avid mouth gently feathered soft kisses along the puckered skin.

"If you're trying to kiss away the pain, where I'm really hurting is just a little bit lower," he told her huskily.

She chuckled, letting her tongue taste, tempt, tease. She heard the sharp intake of his breath, and knew her bold acceptance of his challenge had surprised and aroused him.

She heard the crinkle of plastic as he unwrapped the condom he'd snagged from his pocket before discarding his pants somewhere in the hall, and was grateful he'd had the foresight to think of protection. She let him sheath himself, then kissed her way back up his body, her taut nipples grazing his chest, her hips rocking against his. His hands skimmed over her thighs, his fingers curled around her buttocks, pressing her closer.

She waited for him to press into her, to take control in search of his own pleasure. But he didn't seem to be in any big rush to the finish line. In fact, he seemed more than content just to touch her, tease her, taste her.

Molly endured the exquisite torture for as long as she could, then she straddled his hips, positioning herself so that the tip of his erection was at the juncture of her thighs.

Slowly she lowered herself, moving just the tiniest bit, taking only a fraction of an inch inside of her. Then a little more.

His hands were on her hips, his fingers biting into her flesh. She could feel the tension in him and knew he was fighting against the instinct to drive into her. He was bigger than her, stronger, and they both knew she was only in control at the moment because he wanted her to be, but still, the sense of power was exhilarating.

She continued to tease him, taking him a little bit deeper inside, then drawing back again. His eyes were so dark they were almost black, and they were intently focused on her. Watching her as she watched him.

Watching her as his hands skimmed up her sides to her breasts, as his fingers toyed with her nipples, circling, stroking, squeezing.

Desire curled like a fist deep in her belly, tight, tighter, until she cried out with her release.

It was the signal he'd been waiting for, and his hips jerked off the mattress and he buried himself deep inside of her in one powerful thrust that had her crying out again at the shock of the next climax that ripped through her, leaving her weak and breathless and shattered.

But Eric wasn't finished with her. He held himself perfectly still until her body had stopped shuddering, then he flipped her over, so that she was on her back and he was stretched out on top of her, pressing deep inside of her.

He whispered to her, speaking softly in Spanish. She didn't understand all of the words, but his tone was as sensual as a caress, and just as arousing. He began to move. Slow and deep strokes that touched her very core. Then hard and fast thrusts. Harder. Faster.

She'd thought she was sated. He'd made certain she was satisfied before he'd pursued his own pleasure, and yet, she could feel the desperate, achy need building inside of her again. Her heels dug into the mattress, her nails bit into his shoulders, and her hips matched his frantic rhythm as her desire escalated again until the world dropped away and there was nothing to hold on to but each other.

He collapsed with his head on her pillow, his arm wrapped around her, and his heart beating against hers.

They made love twice more before exhaustion finally overrode passion, and Molly fell into a deep and blissful sleep in the warm comfort of his arms.

She woke up in the morning, cold and alone, and found herself regretting not the hours she'd spent with Eric but that he was already gone.

Chapter Two

"Pregnant?"

Molly stared at the doctor for a minute, then laughed as she shook her head.

"I think you're going to want to run that test again."

Dr. Morgan looked at her with both understanding and compassion in her deep green eyes. She'd been Molly's doctor for more than twenty years, long before her dark hair had become so liberally streaked with grey and the faint lines around her eyes and mouth had multiplied.

"I'll rerun the test," she told her. "If you can look me in the eye and honestly tell me that you haven't had sex in the past two months."

Molly's fingers curled around the edge of the examining table, her damp palms sticking to the paper. "Not unprotected sex."

"Well, I'm glad to hear that," Dr. Morgan said. "But you know there isn't any method of contraception that is one hundred percent effective."

She could only stare at her as the reality of what the doctor was saying began to sink in and her heart began to hammer out its panic against her ribs.

"It was one night," she whispered.

One night after four years of going to bed alone.

"That's all it takes," the doctor said gently.

Molly shook her head, still unwilling to believe what the doctor was saying. "But I don't feel pregnant. I don't feel any different—just tired."

"That's often one of the first signs."

"I haven't been sick."

"Not every woman experiences morning sickness. You might be one of the lucky ones."

Lucky? Molly was too stunned to really know how she was feeling, but she was pretty sure it wasn't lucky.

"That's assuming you want to continue with this pregnancy," Dr. Morgan continued gently. "It is still early and—"

Molly shook her head again. She knew what the doctor was going to say—she was going to tell her there were options. She knew what those options were. She also knew there was only one choice for her—and it was the same choice her own mother had made thirty-one years earlier.

"I'm going to have the baby," she said.

"Do you know the father?" Dr. Morgan asked gently.

Her cheeks burned with shame as Molly realized she probably should have kept her "one night" comment to herself, but she managed to choke out the lie, "Of course."

She knew his name—his first name, anyway. And she knew he was from a country called Tesoro del Mar. And she knew that he kissed like there was no tomorrow and made her feel as no man had ever made her feel before. Beyond that, she knew almost nothing at all.

"If you're going to have this baby, the father should be told," Dr. Morgan said. "This isn't something you should have to go through on your own."

She nodded, because she knew it was true. She also knew that if she somehow managed to track him down, Eric wasn't likely to be thrilled to learn that he'd knocked up some woman he picked up in a bar. And that was the tawdry truth of what had happened between them, even if, at the time, it hadn't seemed tawdry at all.

But the soul-deep connection she'd been certain she'd felt in the darkest hours of the night had been illuminated as to what it really was in the bright light of day—a good healthy dose of lust that temporarily overrode common sense—and a passion that was apparently stronger than latex condoms.

Molly walked from the doctor's office to Celebrations by Fiona. The exclusive boutique was ten blocks from the medical arts building and she was more than halfway there before she questioned the wisdom of undertaking such a stroll in low-heeled sling-backs and ninety-degree heat. But she'd needed some time to think about the news she'd been given and she knew that when she got to Fiona's, she wouldn't have a minute to do so.

Her cousin had established a reputation as one of the premier event planners in Texas and her services were sought by everyone who was anyone in the state. She'd planned the island nuptials of a Cowboys' quarterback, personally oversaw every detail of the small garden wedding for an Oscar-winning actress and co-ordinated the renewal of vows to celebrate the fiftieth anniversary of the governor and his wife.

But it turned out that her most challenging assignment and most demanding client wasn't a celebrity or politician, it was herself. And her mistake, in Molly's opinion, was in not hiring someone else to oversee the details of her own wedding—a wedding at which Molly would be the maid of honor the following month.

It seemed like a lifetime ago that Molly had been shopping for dresses and bouquets of flowers, dreaming of "happily ever after." She'd been so full of hope for her future, eager to marry the man she loved, looking forward to raising a family together.

Though that engagement had fallen apart, she'd still believed that someday she would find someone special to share her life and build a family with. Now she'd skipped over the marriage part and was going straight to motherhood—definitely not her childhood dream but a reality that she would have to deal with it.

First, however, she had to tackle the issue of a bridesmaid dress.

Fiona was hovering just inside the door, waiting for her, when she finally arrived.

"Goodness," she said, noting her cousin's flushed cheeks. "You look like you just finished running a marathon."

"Even a short walk feels like a marathon in this heat," she said, not wanting to admit how far she'd walked or where she'd come from.

Fiona scooped a bottle of water out of the minifridge in her office and handed it to her.

"Thanks." Molly took the bottle and sank into an empty chair. "Have you finally picked a dress for me?"

"Sort of."

Molly arched a brow as she uncapped the water.

Fiona gestured to a garment rack that was crowded with gowns.

Molly stared. "There must be a dozen dresses there."

"Sixteen," her cousin admitted.

"I realize the layered look is in, but sixteen might be a bit excessive."

"I couldn't decide," Fiona said, a trifle defensively.

"Couldn't you at least have narrowed it down?"

"That is narrowed down."

Molly shouldn't have been surprised. Even with all of Fiona's contacts in the industry, it had taken her cousin three weeks and trips to both New York City and San Francisco to finally decide on her own gown—from a local boutique.

"I know that pastels are all the rage for summer weddings," Fiona was explaining now, "but I think jewel tones work better with your coloring and, since you're my only attendant, you can pick whatever you want."

Whatever she wanted so long as it was sapphire, emerald or ruby, Molly noted, and rose from her chair for a closer examination of the gowns.

But as she sorted through the collection, her mind slipped back to another examination, to her conversation with Dr. Morgan and the one word that continued to reverberate inside her head.

Pregnant.

"Any thoughts?" Fiona asked.

I thought I would regret it more if I didn't spend the night with him.

Of course, that thought was immediately followed by a wave of guilt. As much as she hadn't planned to get pregnant at this point in her life, she wouldn't regret the child that she would have. The baby growing inside of her probably wasn't the size of a pea yet, but Molly loved her already.

"Molly?" The prompt drew her attention back to the rack of dresses.

"They all look great," she said, forcing enthusiasm into her voice.

"That's what I thought, too," Fiona told her.

Molly went with her instincts and grabbed a strapless floor-length gown of deep blue silk and slipped through the door. She stripped away her clothes, careful not to look at her refection in any of the mirrors that surrounded her. She didn't want to look at her body, to think about the changes that were happening inside of her—changes that she knew were invisible to the outside world but essential to the tiny life inside her.

She tugged the zipper up, straightened the skirt and stepped back outside to show her friend.

"Oh. Wow." Fiona grinned. "That's it—it's perfect."

Molly exhaled a silent sigh of relief that she would be spared having to model the other fifteen dresses.

"You are going to knock his socks off in that dress," her cousin said.

"Whose socks am I knocking off?" she asked warily.

"The best man's."

Molly wasn't so sure that she wanted to be near any man even taking his socks off, because the last time that happened she'd ended up pregnant. Well, at least she'd had the chance to experience the most amazing sex of her life first. Yeah, it was good to know that she'd discovered a sex drive just in time to put it on the back burner for the next several years while she raised the illegitimate child of a man whose last name she didn't even know.

"I can't wait for you to meet him," Fiona said, for the millionth time since she'd first met her fiancé's childhood best friend. "If I wasn't so in love with Scott…" She deliberately let her words trail off, then grinned. "But I am in love with Scott, so it would be really great if you managed to hook up with him."

"I'm not looking to hook up with anyone," Molly said firmly.

Fiona forged ahead, as if she hadn't even heard her. "I really wished you'd met him when he was here, then you'd know what I'm talking about."

"I'll meet him at the rehearsal," Molly reminded her.

"Are you bringing anyone to the wedding?"

"You know I'm not."

"Because he's not bringing a date, either."

"Fiona," she warned her cousin.

"I'm just saying."

"I know what you're saying. And I know you just want me to find someone as wonderful as Scott, but I'm really not looking to get involved with anyone right now." And probably not for a long time. "There's just too much going on in my life right now to even think about adding the complication of a relationship."

Fiona's eyes narrowed. "What aren't you telling me?"

And that, Molly knew, was the problem of having a cousin who was also her best friend and who knew her better than anyone else in the world. But she shook her head, not ready to share the news with anyone just yet.

"Your wedding is less than a month away," she reminded Fiona. "You should have enough to think about without worrying about my love life."

Her statement succeeded in deflecting her cousin's attention, as she knew it would, and they talked about flowers and music and other details until Fiona's next appointment arrived and Molly was able to escape.

He couldn't get her out of his mind.

Almost two months after he'd returned to Tesoro del Mar, Eric still couldn't stop thinking about Molly Shea. At first, he'd been certain it was just the memories of spectacular sex that haunted his dreams. He'd wanted to believe it was nothing more than that. But as six weeks turned into seven and he still couldn't forget her, he finally admitted it was more than the incredible sensation of her body wrapped around his that kept him awake at night—it was the sparkle in her eyes, the way she smiled, the sound of her laughter.

It was all those memories that plagued his thoughts and made him wonder if he shouldn't have stayed in her bed instead of worrying about his flight home the next morning. But really, what difference would another day or two have made, except maybe to make him even more reluctant to leave the haven of her arms?

Still, he was a prince. He most certainly wasn't going to let himself get tied up in knots over any woman, and especially not an American bartender. But with each day that passed, the memories he'd expected to dim only grew sharper, and the need inside him grew stronger.

Or maybe he just had too much time on his hands.

He'd been at loose ends since the accident that had prematurely ended his naval career, and without any direction or focus. He'd assumed some duties back home, but as important as he knew the royal family was to the country, he wasn't sure he could imagine making a career out of public appearances and shaking hands with foreign diplomats.

His recent conversation with Scott hovered in the back of his mind, but he knew the offer to work at DELconnex wasn't the answer. Or not the whole answer. He wanted something more than a new career. He wanted a wife—a family.

He frowned at that thought. Not that it was unusual for a thirty-six-year-old man to think about settling down, but it was unusual for *him.* On the other hand, nothing had been "usual" for Eric since he'd left the navy, and maybe it was time he gave serious consideration to the thought of marriage.

His brother Rowan hadn't been given the luxury of time before he'd been pressured to find a wife. Hundreds, maybe thousands, of women had put themselves forward as bridal candidates when it became known that the prince regent was required to marry. Rowan had surprised everyone when he'd proposed to the royal nanny rather than a woman with recognizable title and ancestry.

Marcus, his younger brother, had also balked at tradition in choosing his bride, marrying a woman who was a foreigner and a successful business owner. And while there was no doubt that both of his brothers were blissfully happy with their respective wives, Eric had always thought that when the time came for him to marry, he would choose a more traditional kind of wife—someone who understood the role of a royal spouse and would be both suitable and content to fulfill it.

But somehow it was thoughts of a sweet and sexy bartender that hovered in the back of his mind and invaded his dreams. And—seven weeks after a single night together—these thoughts began to cause him serious worry. Never before had he been so preoccupied by a woman. Never before had he yearned so deeply for what he couldn't have.

Being born a prince meant there were few things beyond his grasp, but Molly was one of them. They'd both agreed there would be nothing between them after that night. At the time, it had seemed like a perfect arrangement—one night, no strings. But even as the sun had begun to rise in the morning, Eric had regretted their bargain.

One night hadn't been nearly enough to sate the passion that burned so hotly and fiercely between them. Not when, seven weeks later, just thinking of Molly was enough to make him ache with longing.

He wanted to go back to Texas to see her again, and his friend's upcoming wedding gave him the perfect excuse to do so. Of course, he would have to check in with Rowan first, to ensure there were no pressing matters that required his presence in Tesoro del Mar over the next few weeks.

Having decided he should discuss the matter with his brother, he wasn't surprised when he received a call requesting his presence in the prince regent's office. He was surprised to see Cameron Leandres leaving as he was entering.

"Who's going to get fired for letting our cousin through the front gates?" he asked Rowan.

"No one."

Eric took a seat across from his brother's desk and raised his brows.

"I invited Cameron here to discuss the environmental concerns to be addressed at the summit in Berne next month."

"The summit I'm attending?"

"The summit you were going to attend," Rowan corrected. "I've asked Cameron to take your place."

Eric was genuinely perplexed by this turn of events. "Why?"

"Because you're going to be too busy overseeing the expansion of DELconnex U.S.A. into Europe to give this matter the attention it deserves."

Eric scowled. "I haven't told Scott I'd take the job."

"But you want to."

"How do you even know that he offered it to me?"

"I had to call to decline, with sincere regret, the invitation to Scott and Fiona's wedding because it coincides with the opening of the new youth center in Rio Medio that I've already committed to attending. And while I was talking to him, I asked him what kind of offer he'd made to you this time."

Everyone in the family knew that his friend had been trying to entice Eric to join his company since he first launched DELconnex nearly a decade earlier.

Eric and Scott had been friends since two decades before that, when six-year-old Scott Delsey had come with his family to Tesoro del Mar when his father was appointed U.S. ambassador to the small Mediterranean nation. As ambassador, Thomas

Delsey had spent a lot of time at the palace, frequently with his wife and son. Scott had become friends with all of the princes but had developed a particularly close bond with Eric, who was also six at the time. It was a bond as strong as any of blood, and that had endured even after the ambassador had finished his ten-year term and returned with his family to the United States. Eric and Scott had gone to the same college and though they'd later gone their separate ways in life, they'd always remained in touch.

"It's a tempting offer," Rowan said now.

"I've resisted temptation before," Eric told him, even as memories of his trip to Texas taunted him with the knowledge that he'd also succumbed to temptation—and quite happily.

"Why are you thinking of resisting?" his brother asked, and it took Eric a moment to haul his mind out of Molly's bed and back to their conversation.

"Because you need me here."

"I need a minister of international relations, and I think Cameron is well-suited to the position."

"There was a time when he thought he was well-suited to your position, and tried to take it from you," Eric felt compelled to remind him.

"That was six years ago."

"Do you really think he's changed?"

"I think I'd rather know what he's doing than have to guess at it."

Which Eric thought was a valid point. But he was still uneasy about his brother's decision to give any real authority to their cousin—or maybe he was just feeling guilty that Rowan's plan would allow him to do what he wanted when Rowan hadn't been given the same choice.

"I've neglected my duties to this family for too many years already," he protested.

"I probably can't count the number of diplomatic dinners and political photo ops you skipped over the past dozen years," the prince regent admitted. "But those were more than balanced out by the fact that you were serving your country."

Eric was uncomfortable with the admiration and pride he heard in Rowan's voice because he knew his service hadn't been any greater than that of any of his brothers. "Which is no more than you did by giving up your life in London when Julian died, and coming home to run the country and raise his children. And you still do the diplomatic dinners and political photo ops, and more than anyone probably even knows."

"It hasn't all been a hardship," Rowan said, with a smile that told Eric his brother was thinking of his wife and their family.

Eric lowered himself into the chair facing his brother's. "How did you know Lara was the right woman for you?"

"I didn't at first," he admitted. "Or maybe I did but refused to admit it, because I knew getting involved with the royal nanny would create a situation fraught with complications. And it wasn't so much that she was the right woman as she was the *only* woman—the only one I couldn't get out of my mind, the only one I wanted to be with for the rest of my life."

"The only one who would put up with him, more likely," Lara said from behind him.

Eric glanced at his sister-in-law, who was standing in the doorway with a ten-month-old baby tucked under one arm and a three-and-a-half-year-old holding her other hand. Her strawberry-blond hair looked a little more tousled than usual, and there was a stain on the shoulder of her blouse that he knew was courtesy of the baby, but despite the lateness of the hour and the obvious busyness of her day, her smile was still vibrant and beautiful.

Rowan had definitely lucked out when he'd fallen in love with Lara Brennan, Eric thought, with just the slightest twinge of envy. As Marcus had also done when he'd stopped by a little café in West Virginia and met—and eventually fallen in love with—Jewel Callahan. As Eric hoped he might luck out someday and find his own soul mate.

Unbidden, thoughts of Molly again nudged at his mind, but he pushed them aside.

"And I will forever be grateful for that," Rowan said, smiling back at his wife.

"You can prove it by tackling the bedtime routine with a stubborn three-year-old," she told him.

"It would be my pleasure," Rowan said, holding out his arms to the little boy, who went rushing into them.

Eric had to smile at the obvious bond between father and son. It was hard to believe that when Rowan had taken on the responsibility for Julian and Catherine's three children he had almost no experience with—and even less knowledge about—raising kids. Now Christian was seventeen and about to start college in the fall, Lexi was thirteen with a maturity well beyond her years and Damon was nine and still reveling in the joys of childhood and wreaking havoc on the household. Since their marriage, Lara and Rowan had added two of their own, and Rowan had not only embraced fatherhood but managed to juggle his various responsibilities to reflect his commitment to his family.

Eric wasn't really surprised by the apparent ease of his older brother's transition from footloose financier to responsible prince regent. Rowan had always taken his obligations seriously. More surprising to Eric was that his younger brother had willingly made similar changes in his life. He'd never seen Marcus look happier than when he was with Jewel and their baby daughter.

It was at the baptism for young Princess Isabella that Eric was first confronted by the emptiness of his life. Up until then, he'd never thought about what was missing. Or maybe it was more accurate to say that nothing seemed to be missing because his career had fulfilled him so completely.

Over the past three years, he'd had too much time to think, too much time to wonder if there should be something more, although he hadn't really thought about his restless yearning for more in terms of a relationship until he'd met Molly.

"Bath time and story?" Rowan's question to his son drew Eric's attention back to the scene in the library.

"Story!" Matthew repeated with enthusiasm.

"*After* the bath," his mother interjected firmly.

Matthew scowled as Rowan rose with him in his arms.

Eric chuckled. "What is it about little boys that makes them inherently allergic to bathwater?"

"I was hoping you could tell me," Lara said, crossing the room to settle into the chair her husband had vacated. The baby rubbed his face on his mother's shoulder, then popped his thumb in his mouth and snuggled in with a sigh.

Eric felt an unexpected pang as he watched Lara cuddle her infant son. Children were something else he hadn't thought much about because he'd never been in a position to be a father, but spending time with his brothers' children had changed that, too. He wanted a family of his own—a wife and children to come home to at the end of the day, to make plans and share dreams with and to simply *be* with.

Dios, that sounded pathetic, as if he couldn't endure his own company. Or maybe he'd just been enduring his own company for too long. After unsuccessful romances, it had seemed easier to accept solitude than yet another relationship failure. But maybe it was finally time to reconsider that position.

"You and Rowan sure do make beautiful babies," he commented to his sister-in-law now.

Lara smiled. "As much as I want to take credit, the dark hair and eyes are trademark Santiago."

"But Matthew has your mouth and your smile, and William's bone structure is just like yours."

"Do you think so?" She seemed pleased that he would notice such details.

"As I said, you make beautiful babies."

"And you're a flatterer as much as both of your brothers," she mused. "So what deep conversation between you and Rowan did I interrupt?"

"Nothing deep," he assured her.

"You've met a woman," she guessed.

He stared at her, baffled.

She laughed, and automatically rubbed the baby's back when he started to stir. "I heard you ask your brother how he knew I was the right woman for him—it wasn't much of a stretch to think that you've met someone who has you thinking in those terms."

"I've just been thinking a lot about my life and my future," he hedged. "And I wanted to tell Rowan about my plan to go back to Texas. It occurred to me that, as the best man, I should be available to help Scott with anything that needs to be done in the last few weeks before the wedding."

Lara's smile was just a little smug. "She's in Texas, isn't she?"

"Whatever you want to believe," he said, knowing it was pointless to deny it.

The widening of her smile only proved she knew she was right. "When are you leaving?"

Chapter Three

Molly pulled a brush through her hair and wrapped an elastic band around it to hold the heavy mass off of her neck. It was only the end of May, not even officially summer yet, but even three days of almost steady rain had done little to alleviate the humidity and forecasters were warning that the season was going to be a brutal one.

As she stripped out of her shorts and T-shirt to change for work, she thought she could use a change of scenery and a break from the oppressive heat—a week or two away from the never-ending problems at home. And she found herself wondering what the weather was like in Tesoro del Mar, if the summers were hot or if there were cool ocean breezes to regulate the temperature.

She wondered if Eric lived somewhere on the coast or in a crowded apartment in the city—or even if there were cities in Tesoro del Mar. She didn't really know anything about the country, or even how big it was, and she didn't know—if she decided to take a trip to the island, as she'd been thinking she might do—if there was any chance her path would cross with his.

It was a crazy idea—almost as crazy as spending the night with a man she didn't know—and yet it was an idea that refused to be discarded.

She'd thought about him a lot since that single night they'd spent together, and not just since she'd learned that she was carrying his child.

But five days after her appointment with Dr. Morgan, she'd still made no effort to find her baby's father and she knew it was past time she did so. She had plenty of legitimate excuses for the delay—including the hundred-and-one daily tasks that kept her at the restaurant for ten or more hours a day.

But the truth was, not one of those things had made her forget about the child she carried or the obligation she had to notify her baby's father. She just didn't know how she was going to track him down.

She booted up the computer and considered what she knew about Eric. Beyond his name, she knew that he lived in a country called Tesoro del Mar and that he'd been in the navy. It wasn't much, but at least it was a start.

A swarm of butterflies winged around in her stomach as she logged onto the Internet and typed the words *"Tesoro del Mar," "Eric"* and *"naval accident"* into the search engine.

She'd barely clicked Enter when the results filled the page.

Tesorian Navy News. Coast Guard Newsletter. Navy News—International Edition. MedSeaSecurityReport. Royal Watch. Naval Briefs. The Spanish Sailor.

She clicked on the first result, scanned the headline.

Prince Eric Injured in Naval Training Accident.

Prince Eric?

Definitely not the right Eric, she decided, and started to close the document when she noted the photo a little bit farther down on the page.

Her breath caught and her brow furrowed as she leaned closer to the screen for a better look.

It *was* him.

Her heart started to beat harder, faster.

She skimmed the article, barely noting any details of the accident that had resulted in the end of his career. Nothing seemed to matter beyond the title that jumped out at her from beneath his picture. "First Officer Prince Eric Santiago."

It occurred to her that maybe "prince" wasn't a royal title but a naval title. It certainly seemed a more feasible explanation than a member of a royal family wandering into her restaurant—and ending up in her bed.

She tried a different search this type, entering only *"prince eric"* and *"tesoro del mar."*

Again, the results were almost instantaneous, and her hand trembled as she clicked on "theroyalhouseofsantiago."

The site opened to a home page that showed a stunning castle of gleaming white stone in front of a backdrop of brilliant blue sky. She clicked on a link labeled "Members of the Royal Family," which popped up a row of photos with names and links beneath them—one of which was Eric, "Principe de la Ciudad del Norte."

She stared at the image, stunned by this confirmation that Eric wasn't just a guy in a bar—he was a member of the royal family of Tesoro del Mar.

She'd slept with a prince.

And now she was pregnant with his child.

She had to tell him—the logical, rational part of her brain wouldn't let her consider anything else. And now she knew where to find him, though she couldn't imagine that she'd simply be permitted to walk up to the front door of the royal palace and announce that she was carrying the prince's baby.

She couldn't think about this right now—just the thought made her head spin.

Pushing away from the desk, she grabbed her cell phone before heading downstairs to make sure the restaurant was set up for dinner. She noticed the voice mail icon on the display and sighed as she dialed into her mailbox, determined to ignore whatever crisis had her sister tracking her down now. But it wasn't Abbey's number on the display, it was Fiona's, and her cousin's voice was quiet and muffled, as if she was trying not to cry.

Fiona wasn't prone to dramatics, so her brief and teary "the wedding's off" message had Molly detouring through the restaurant only long enough to make sure that Karen could stay behind the bar until she returned. As she drove the familiar route to her cousin's ranch, it occurred to her that whatever had Fiona in a panic, it had succeeded in taking Molly's mind off of Prince Eric Santiago.

At least for the moment.

When Eric contacted Scott's fiancée to let her know that he was coming back to San Antonio, Fiona promised that a room would be ready for him and chatted excitedly about the final preparations for the wedding. But something happened between the time of his phone call and his arrival at the door so that she was no longer bubbling over with happiness but with tears.

Having spent most of his adult life in the navy, Eric felt completely out of his element when confronted by a weeping woman. Not that it was his job to comfort his friend's fiancée—and thank God Scott was there to do that—but he still felt helpless. And clueless.

"We got a call from the manager of Harcourt Castle," Scott

explained, when Fiona's sobs had quieted enough that conversation was possible.

"That's where the wedding's going to be, right?"

His friend gave a small shake of his head as he continued to pat Fiona's back consolingly. "We've had a lot of rain over the past couple of days and some of the lower lying areas experienced flooding, including Harcourt."

Eric knew a flood indicated water damage, which meant the venue was likely out of commission for several months—definitely past the date of the wedding.

"Maybe it's a sign," Fiona sniffed.

"It's not a sign," Scott soothed his bereft fiancée. "Except for the fact that we'll need to find another location for the wedding."

She brushed her tears away and looked up at him, incredulous. "Less than a month before the date?"

For the first time since Eric had arrived on the scene, Scott looked uncertain. "Does that seem unlikely?"

"Not unlikely—" the tears began falling again, her words barely comprehensible "—impossible. And—" she gulped in a breath "—you know why I wanted the castle."

"We met at Harcourt," Scott explained to Eric.

"And he took me back there to ask me to marry him," Fiona said, suddenly sobbing harder.

Yeah, Eric was definitely out of his element, and desperately wracked his brain for a solution—any solution—to stop the tears.

"Okay, so we'll postpone the wedding for a few months," Scott suggested.

"We've already sent out the invitations, ordered the cake, the flowers and—"

"I said postpone," her fiancé interjected, "not cancel."

She sighed. "It seems like we've been waiting so long already, and I just want to be married to you."

"Then let's do it," Scott said impulsively. "Let's forget all the chaos and crises, hop onto a plane to Vegas and get married."

Fiona's nose wrinkled. "Vegas?"

"I know it's not what we'd planned, but we can have a big, blowout reception back here in a few months, when Harcourt Castle is reopened."

His fiancée still hesitated.

Eric had never been to Vegas, but he'd seen enough movies to form an impression of the city and he could understand Fiona's reluctance. She wanted ambience and elegance, and what Scott was offering was loud and garish. Okay, maybe that wasn't an entirely fair assessment considering that he'd never stepped foot in the town, but he thought he'd gotten to know his friend's fiancée well enough during his last visit to be certain it wasn't what she'd envisioned.

"Vegas," she said again, more contemplative than critical this time.

He figured it was a testament to how much Fiona loved Scott that she was even considering it.

"Or you could hop on a plane to a picturesque island in the Mediterranean and have a quiet ceremony on the beach and an intimate reception at the royal palace," Eric offered as an alternative.

The future bride and groom swiveled their heads in his direction.

"Could we?" Scott asked.

"You said it was a small wedding?"

"Fifty-two guests," his friend confirmed.

"We'd need to charter a plane but otherwise, there shouldn't be any problem. So long as there's nothing going on at the palace on that date, we could fly everyone in a few days early for a brief vacation on the island, then have the wedding as planned on Saturday."

Fiona glanced from Eric to Scott and back again. "That sounds awfully expensive," she said, but the sparkle was back in her eyes, revealing her enthusiasm.

"It would be my wedding gift to you," Eric told her.

"A Crock-Pot is a wedding gift," she said. "What you're offering is…a dream."

He shrugged. "You make my best friend happy. If this makes you happy, it's a fair trade."

Her smile was radiant. "Then I'll say 'thank you.' But we'll stick with Scott's plan to hold a formal reception back here in a few months and just have immediate family for the ceremony in Tesoro del Mar. And Molly, my maid of honor, of course."

When Molly arrived at the ranch, she was both surprised and immensely relieved to learn that the crisis had already been diverted.

"I didn't think anything could be more romantic than being married at Harcourt House," Fiona gushed, all smiles instead of tears now. "But a wedding at a royal palace might just top everything else."

Molly sank down onto the arm of a chair. "A royal palace?"

"Scott's in the other room with Eric now, confirming the arrangements."

The butterflies were swarming again.

Eric. The best man. The friend of Scott's that Fiona had been talking about for months who somehow had access to a royal palace. Could it be—

No. It wasn't possible. She'd just been so unnerved by the realization that her baby's father was a prince that she was jumping to conclusions. Because as much as her cousin had talked about the best man, Fiona had never mentioned that he was royalty. Molly *definitely* would have remembered that.

She managed to smile. “So where is this royal palace?”

“It’s on an island in the Mediterranean called Tesoro del Mar. I’d never even heard of it before I met Eric, and I didn’t even know he was a prince until a few days ago. Scott said they’ve been friends for so long he doesn’t think about the fact that Eric is in line for the throne, but I nearly fainted when I found out. Can you believe the best man at my wedding is a prince?”

“Unbelievable,” Molly agreed, as thoughts and questions whipped around in her mind like dry leaves in a hurricane. And before she could grasp hold of even one of them, he was there.

He was standing in front of her—okay, across the room, but the distance did nothing to dilute the effect of his presence. His legs were as long as she remembered, his shoulders as broad, his jaw as strong, his eyes as dark.

Yes, she remembered all of the details—the thickness of his hair, the curve of his lips, the skill of his hands. But she hadn’t quite remembered—maybe hadn’t let herself remember—how completely fascinating he was as a whole.

He smiled at Fiona. “Everything’s confirmed.”

She threw her arms around his neck. “Oh, thank you, Eric. You’re the best.”

“That’s why he’s the best man,” Scott said, unconcerned by the fact that his fiancée was embracing another man. Eric chuckled.

The sound of that laugh, warm and rich and familiar, sent shivers down her spine, tingles to her center.

It was Scott who spotted Molly first, and he smiled. “Hey, Molly.”

Eric’s head turned. His gaze locked on hers, and widened in shock.

Molly thought she had some idea just how he felt.

“Eric—” Scott turned to his friend “—you haven’t met Molly yet, have you?”

"No, we haven't," Molly answered before he could, rising to her feet and praying that her wobbly legs would support her.

"But I've certainly heard a lot about her," Eric said, his eyes never leaving Molly's face.

She definitely hadn't remembered everything—like how one look could make her pulse race and her knees quiver, as her pulse was racing and her knees were quivering now.

"And here she is," Scott said. And to Molly, "This is His Royal Highness, Prince Eric Santiago of Tesoro del Mar."

"Should I curtsy?" she asked lightly.

"No need," he said.

She didn't actually remember offering her hand, but she found it engulfed in his, cradled in his warmth. It was a simple handshake—there was nothing at all inappropriate about it. And yet she felt her cheeks heat, her skin burn, as memories of his hands on her body assaulted her mind from every direction.

The heat in his eyes told her that he was also remembering, and though her mind warned her to back away, her body yearned to shift close, closer.

"It's a pleasure to see you, Molly," he said in that low, sexy voice that had whispered much more intimately and explicitly in her ear as they'd rolled around on her bed together.

"Oh, we're going to have so much fun together in Tesoro del Mar," Fiona said, then to Molly, "You will come, won't you?"

A wedding on a Mediterranean island sounded romantic enough, throw in a royal palace, and Molly could understand why her cousin was glowing with excitement and anticipation. And no matter how much Molly's brain warned that going to Tesoro del Mar was a very bad idea—that going anywhere with Eric Santiago was a very bad idea—she couldn't refuse something that meant so much to Fiona.

So she ignored the knots in her stomach and forced a bright

smile. "Of course I'll be there. You can hardly get married without your maid of honor."

Fiona threw her arms around Molly, just as she'd done with Eric, and hugged her tight. "Oh, thank you, thank you, thank you."

Molly hugged her back. "I just want your wedding to be perfect for you."

"It will be now," her cousin said confidently.

Molly was pleased that Fiona's problems were solved, but couldn't help but think her own had just multiplied.

It had been unsettling enough to accept that she was pregnant with a stranger's baby, but learning that the stranger was her cousin's fiancé's best friend added a whole other layer of complications. And she couldn't help but wonder how differently everything might have played out if she'd known two months ago what she knew now about *Prince* Eric Santiago.

"Okay, now that the crisis has been resolved, I should get back to work," Molly said, eager to make her escape.

But she felt the heat of Eric's gaze on her as she made her way to the door, and acknowledged that this new information might not have changed anything. Because even now, she wanted him as much as she'd wanted him then.

This time, however, she was determined to prove stronger than the desire he stirred inside of her.

At least, she hoped she would.

Chapter Four

Molly *knew* Eric would show up at her door the next morning. She only hoped to have a cup of coffee in her system before she had to face him again—a hope that was obliterated when the knock sounded just as she was measuring grinds into the filter. She set the basket into place, pressed the button and went to respond to his knock.

He was dressed casually in a pair of jeans and a collared T-shirt, much as he'd been the first night he walked into the bar. And though he looked better than any man had a right to look, there certainly wasn't anything about his appearance or his attire that warned he was a prince. And even now, even knowing all the details she'd learned from the Internet, she found it difficult to think of him as royalty. She could only remember that he was a man—a man she'd taken to her bed and with whom she'd shared intimacies and pleasures she'd never before imagined.

"Good morning," he said.

To which she responded with a barely civil, "Come in."

"A little out of sorts this morning?"

"I work nights," she reminded him. "The hours before noon aren't my best time."

"Should I come back?"

She shook her head. "We might as well just get this over with."

His lips quirked. "What, exactly, are we getting over?"

"The awkward morning-after conversation that we managed to avoid the morning after." She reached into the cupboard for two mugs, filled both with coffee, then slid one across the table to him.

He'd drank black coffee at the bar that night, she remembered, which was good because she didn't have any cream. She dumped a generous spoonful of sugar into her own cup and stirred. She planned to make the switch to decaf soon, but the doctor had assured her a couple of cups a day wouldn't hurt the baby and she needed the caffeine right now.

"Well, you could explain why you didn't want Scott and Fiona to know we'd met before."

"Because they would have had questions about how and when, and I wasn't sure how to answer." She sipped her coffee, felt it churn uneasily in her stomach.

"How about the truth?"

"The whole truth?"

"I'm not ashamed of what happened between us. We're both adults, we were attracted to one another, we acted upon that attraction."

"I don't do one night stands with strangers," she told him.

"I seem to recall you telling me that already—right before you invited me back to your apartment."

She felt her cheeks flush at the reminder—or maybe it was the heat in his gaze that was causing her own body temperature to rise. She wasn't in the habit of having sex with men she barely knew, and she'd *never* had sex with a man she'd met only a few hours earlier. But she'd let herself give in to the yearning because she never expected to see him again.

It was supposed to be a crazy, once-in-a-lifetime impulse, a chance to prove to herself that she could be wild and spontaneous and not tie herself up in knots about it forever after. Except that it turned out to be a crazy, once-in-a-lifetime impulse that was going to have some major, long-term repercussions.

Repercussions Prince Eric still didn't know about.

"Just because I slept with you once doesn't mean I'll do so again just because circumstances have thrown us together and it's convenient."

He smiled at her across the table—a smile that made all of her bones turn to jelly and made her grateful she was sitting down.

"I wasn't thinking about the convenience factor so much as the it-was-really-great-sex factor."

"The only reason I made an exception to my rule was because I didn't expect to ever see you again."

"I didn't think I'd ever see you again, either," he admitted. "And yet, you've been on my mind almost constantly over the past few weeks, and it was always my plan upon returning to Texas to find you."

"That wasn't our agreement," she reminded him.

"So let's make a new agreement."

"What do you propose—lots of hot sex in the few weeks leading up to Scott and Fiona's wedding, after which I go back to serving drinks and you go back to doing whatever it is a royal does?"

Something in her tone must have given her away, because his brows lifted. "You're annoyed that I didn't tell you I'm a prince," he guessed.

"Do you think?"

"Why don't I remember your affinity for sarcasm?"

"Maybe because we really didn't know one another at all before we fell into bed together."

"Are you saying your decision to sleep with me would have been different if you'd know I was a prince?"

"Yes," she asserted vehemently.

"Why?"

"Because then I would have known that I meant nothing more to you than another conquest in another town."

Even as she spoke the words, she realized how hypocritical they sounded. After all, she was the one who'd insisted that a one night stand was all she wanted.

But he didn't point out this fact. Instead he said, "You were never a conquest. You were a beautiful woman who intrigued me as no woman has done in a very long time."

She wanted to believe him, but she couldn't get past the fact that he was a prince and she'd been rejected by too many average guys to believe that she could have captured the attention of someone so extraordinary.

"I'm not going to sleep with you again."

He lifted his cup to his lips, drank. "I got the impression, when Fiona asked you about coming to Tesoro del Mar, that you wanted to refuse."

"It's not that I wanted to," she denied. "It's just not a great time for me to be leaving the country."

"Is that the truth? Or is it that you didn't want to be with me?"

"You weren't a factor in my decision," she lied.

"No?" he challenged softly and, reaching across the table, brushed his knuckles down her cheek.

The gentle caress sent tingles down her spine, and when she responded with another no, it sounded almost like a sigh.

He smiled. "Well, I'm glad you are coming. Tesoro del Mar is a beautiful country, and I will look forward to showing it to you."

"I'm going for Fiona, not for a vacation."

"There's no reason you can't do both."

She shook her head. "I really can't be away from my business for too long."

"You don't have a manager?"

"*I'm* the manager."

"But you don't work every single shift," he guessed.

"No," she admitted. Karen had shared the managerial duties for a few years now, usually covering the dinner shift so that Molly had a break between lunch and evening duties and could take the occasional day off. "But I'm never too far away if there's a problem."

"Is it that you don't trust your manager to take care of things in your absence?" he wondered. "Or that you don't trust yourself to be alone with me?"

"There's nothing wrong with your ego, is there?"

He only grinned. "I don't recall you having complaints about my ego—or any of my other parts—when we were together."

No—there had definitely been no reason to complain and no ability to do so when she was writhing and moaning with pleasure.

"Are we finished here?" she asked, deliberately ignoring his comment. "Because I have to be downstairs for a delivery in about ten minutes."

He pushed his chair away from the table. "Fiona will let you know the travel arrangements."

"Thanks." She followed him to the door.

He stepped out onto the landing, then pivoted back to face her again. "And the answer to your question is no—we're not even close to being finished here."

* * *

Molly was in a mood when she went down to the bar and she knew it. She was tired and she was cranky and it was all Eric's fault. As if it wasn't enough to find out that the man she'd picked up in her own bar was a prince, now he'd suddenly reappeared in her life, wanting to pick up right where they left off.

Of course, he didn't know that the last time they'd gotten naked and horizontal together, they'd made a baby. She was certain that little bit of information would make him reconsider his pursuit of her, but she definitely wasn't ready to share.

You have to tell him.

She sighed even as she cursed the nagging voice of her conscience. She *knew* she had to tell him. She *would* tell him. Just not yet. Not until she was feeling a little less flustered and emotional about everything.

Okay—that might take a little longer than the seven months remaining before her due date, so maybe that wasn't a reasonable guideline.

After the wedding, she decided. She would be close to the end of the first trimester by then and there wouldn't be any reason for them to remain in contact afterward if he didn't want to.

She nodded, satisfied with that reasoning. "After the wedding."

"What wedding?"

She hadn't realized she'd spoken the thought out loud until Dave, the delivery man from the local liquor store responded with the question.

She scrawled her name on the bill he presented to her and shook her head. "I'm babbling to myself. Obviously I've got too much on my mind."

"My brother talks to himself all the time," Dave told her. "My mother thinks he's a genius. My dad just thinks he's nuts."

"There's probably a fine line there," Molly said.

"Which side do you fall on?" he asked curiously.

"Nuts," she said. "Definitely certifiably insane."

She had to be if she was still attracted to a man who'd messed up every single aspect of her life.

"Admitting a problem is the first step toward getting help," he said, and winked at her.

She restocked the shelf behind the bar, then carried the extra inventory to the storage room. The boxes were heavy, and though the weight wasn't anything she couldn't handle right now, she knew there would come a time when she would have to stop that kind of lifting. She wouldn't do anything that would jeopardize the well-being of her child.

But, as she stifled another yawn, she found herself worrying that she might already be jeopardizing her baby's well-being. She was tired—physically and mentally exhausted. Was that normal in the first few months of pregnancy? Or were the erratic hours at the restaurant taking an additional toll on her body?

She'd had to drag herself out of bed this morning, and she'd turned the shower spray to cool to jolt herself awake. What she'd told Eric was true—she'd never been at her best in the mornings, but she wasn't usually so grumpy.

Even when she'd been in high school and had to get up for classes in the morning, she often worked late to help her dad. When she was a teen, he'd been strict about keeping her away from the bar, but when the last customer was gone and the door was locked at the end of the night, she would come out of the kitchen to help him with the clean-up of the restaurant and the close-out of the register and anything else that needed to be done.

She'd loved that time of night, the quiet camaraderie they'd shared. Just thinking about it now, she felt an aching emptiness inside. Her father had been gone for almost ten years now, but there still wasn't a day that went by that she didn't think about him and how much she missed him.

He'd been in her thoughts even more than usual recently, and she wondered if that was because she so desperately wanted to tell someone about the baby she carried. She knew her father would have been disappointed about the circumstances of her pregnancy, but he would have been thrilled about the child. Family had always been the most important part of life to James Shea, with even the bar running a distance second.

When his wife bailed on him after fifteen years of marriage, he'd raised his daughters alone, and he'd raised them with love and compassion. If he'd had one regret, it was that Maureen had cut all ties when she'd walked out. He felt it was important for children to have the love of both parents, and he always lamented the fact that he couldn't give that to his daughters.

He wouldn't approve of Molly's decision not to tell Eric about her pregnancy, of that she had no doubt. Not that she wasn't ever going to tell him, she reminded that nagging voice in the back of her mind, just that she needed some more time to assimilate what she'd learned about her baby's father before she told him he was going to be a father.

She thought about how her dad would react to that bit of information.

"You always were my princess," he would have said with a smile. "And now you'll have the title to prove it."

Because he would also assume that, being pregnant with Eric's baby, she would marry him—whether or not it was what either of them wanted. Yes, family was important to James Shea, and so was responsibility, as he'd proven when he married Molly's mother after learning that she was carrying his child.

But that was thirty-one years ago, and even if Eric offered marriage as a solution, she knew it wasn't one she could accept. It certainly wasn't a solution that had worked for her parents. Not that they hadn't tried—at least for a while. But in the end,

Maureen Shea had woke up one morning and, looking around, decided she didn't like what her life had become and walked away from everything.

Molly didn't think she would ever understand how a woman could walk away from her child like that—cutting all ties and never looking back. Instinctively, her hand went to her still-flat tummy. Though her baby was just starting to be, she was already overwhelmed with love for her child and she vowed silently but vehemently to always be there for her baby.

Which meant that she had to start giving serious consideration to the day-to-day practicalities of parenthood. In particular, she needed to consider what was she going to do when she had a child of her own—could she continue to serve customers with a playpen behind the bar? And even if that worked for the first several months, she couldn't keep a toddler confined to a mesh-cage for a six-hour shift any more than she could allow him free rein to crawl around the restaurant.

But what other option did she have?

Sell.

The answer popped into her head from nowhere—or maybe it had been lurking in the back of her mind since Abbey had first spoken of the possibility after their father died.

Her sister had broached the subject a few more times since then, but Molly had always balked. Shea's was their legacy, the only thing they had left that was their father's.

And even if they sold the bar, even if they found a buyer, what would she do after? Who would hire her? She had no real skills, no experience, and now she had a baby on the way.

You could write.

This time the voice in head sounded suspiciously like her grandmother's, and the words were a familiar refrain.

Even as a child, she'd had stories in her head. Her father had enjoyed the fanciful tales she'd spun and appreciated that her narratives entertained his customers; her grandmother had always insisted that Molly was a born storyteller. Molly only knew that there were characters and scenes constantly spinning around in her mind and she had a drawerful of notebooks in which she'd jotted down those ideas in an attempt to clear them from her mind.

But while she might occasionally fantasize about being a writer, she didn't have any illusions that she could simply decide to make that kind of career change and expect to pay the bills. So what could she do?

She felt the sting of tears in her eyes as the questions came at her from all directions. Questions without apparent answers. Problems without any solutions.

She sat on a stool and pressed the heels of her hands to her eyes and wished again that her father was here. Since he'd passed away, she'd been the mature and responsible one—the one everyone else turned to for help, the shoulder that others cried on. For once—just once—she wanted a shoulder to cry on, strong arms to wrap around her, someone she could count on and believe in and—

She shook her head, furiously pushing aside the image of Eric Santiago that managed to steal into her mind. How could she even think about leaning on him when he was the one who'd started her world spinning out of control? She couldn't. No way, no how.

Molly would handle this current predicament as she'd handled everything else in her life since her father died—on her own.

Eric managed to stay away from the restaurant and the temptation of Molly for three days. On day four, he decided he wanted to go out for lunch, and found himself driving toward Shea's. She was right in saying that they didn't know one another very well, but what he found more interesting than this assertion was her determination to keep him at a distance so that she wouldn't get to know him.

This time when he entered the restaurant, he saw Molly not standing behind the bar but seated at it, talking to another woman beside her. He wasn't going to interrupt, but it was almost as if she was as attuned to his presence as he was to hers, because she looked up and her eyes met his.

He smiled, and she smiled back, albeit tentatively.

As if cluing in to the silent exchange, the woman seated beside Molly looked up. The two women looked enough alike that he would have guessed they were sisters, though he hadn't known that she had a sister, which again proved her point that there was a lot they didn't know about one another.

Molly was wearing slim-fitting jeans and a sleeveless blouse with tiny little flowers embroidered on the collar. Practical yet feminine, he thought, and so perfectly suited to Molly. Her sister was wearing a dress with a criss-cross tie down the back that drew attention to her curves and strappy sandals with pencil-thin heels. Her hair wasn't as long or as dark as Molly's and was streaked with lighter strands.

His gaze moved back to Molly, noting the hair that was pulled away from her face in a ponytail, the deep blue eyes surrounded by thick dark lashes, full lips that were slicked with clear gloss, and he felt the now-familiar stir of desire low in his belly.

"Just in the neighborhood?" Molly asked.

"Just hungry," he said. "And I heard they serve a pretty good lunch in here."

"You heard right," Molly said. Then, at the nudge from her sister, she made the introductions.

"This is my sister, Abbey," she told him. Then to Abbey, "Meet Prince Eric Santiago."

"*Prince* Eric?"

"Scott's best friend," Molly explained to her sister.

"The best man," Abbey said, and lifted a brow. "And are you? The best, I mean."

Eric looked at Molly, who rolled her eyes.

"You're married," she reminded her sister.

"Separated," Abbey said.

"And Eric came in for a meal, not an interrogation." Molly stood and, grabbing a menu from the counter, led him to a booth in the corner.

"I wouldn't mind some company," he said, sliding into the booth.

"You want me to send my sister over?"

"I meant *your* company," he clarified.

"Sorry, I have to finish up next week's schedule."

He hadn't really expected that she would accept his invitation.

For reasons he couldn't even begin to fathom, she was edgy around him, almost antagonistic. Instead of dissuading him, her attitude only made him all the more determined to break through her barriers and rediscover the warm, wonderful woman he knew was inside.

"You could do that here—unless you think I'm too much of a distraction."

"You're just too much."

He grinned. "I'll take that as a compliment."

"You would." She dropped the menu on the table, then with a sigh, she slid into the seat across from him. "You have a way of irritating me so that I forget I'm trying to be nice."

"Why does it take such an effort?"

"Because you rub me the wrong way."

He let his eyes rake over her, in a slow and very hot perusal, before he said, "That's not how I remember it."

She huffed out a breath. "You see? That's exactly what I'm talking about. I'm attempting to have a normal conversation and you keep throwing out these little references to a night I'm trying to forget."

"Why are you trying to forget?"

"Because it's over and done and it's not going to happen again."

"It seems to me that if forgetting is such an effort, it's not nearly as over and done as you want to believe."

She drew in a deep breath, expelled it slowly, deliberately.

"I wanted to say that hosting the wedding in Tesoro del Mar is an incredibly kind and generous thing to do."

"And you're surprised that I can be kind and generous?" he couldn't resist teasing.

"No," she said. "I'm just trying to thank you for turning what could have been a disaster into a celebration."

"My motives aren't entirely noble."

"No?"

"I want to spend time with you, Molly, and you'll have a lot fewer excuses to avoid me when we're in Tesoro del Mar."

"You made the offer before you even knew I was Fiona's maid of honor," she pointed out.

"Guilty," he admitted. "But that doesn't mean I'm not willing to take advantage of the fact."

"I'm flattered by your interest, Eric, really. But I'm not looking for a relationship right now."

"Why not?"

"My reasons aside, I can't believe you're looking to get involved with a bartender."

"I'm not a snob, Molly."

"But you're a prince, and I can't imagine a foreigner with neither a title nor a fortune would ever be a suitable companion—even temporarily—for a royal."

He couldn't help but smile at that. "Both of my sisters-in-law used to think the same way. Lara was an Irish nanny. Jewel was an American horse trainer."

"And your point?"

"Well, I'm not asking you to marry me."

She responded to his assurance with a small smile, and he felt another tug inside. It was warmer and softer than desire, but somehow stronger, too. And he realized he would do almost anything to earn another one of those smiles, for more quiet moments like this one.

"But when we get to the island," he continued, "I might ask to show you around."

She studied him for a moment, those deep blue eyes considering, before she said, "And if you ask nicely, I just might say yes." Then she slid out of the booth. "Enjoy your lunch."

As Eric watched her walk away, appreciating the way worn denim molded to a nicely toned derriere, he was pleased with her response. It was a small step forward, but after so many in retreat, at least it was progress.

Chapter Five

Abbey came into the kitchen the next day and sat by the prep counter to watch Molly chop carrots and celery into sticks. For her sister to show up at the restaurant two days in a row was unusual, and Molly found herself wondering if Abbey had come in to see her or hoping to see Eric again—a question that was answered when Abbey said, “Jason came home last night.”

Molly stopped chopping to look at her sister, trying to decide if this was good news, trying not to resent the fact that her sister didn’t see anything wrong with asking for advice about her marriage to the man she’d stolen from Molly.

“Do you want to reconcile?” she asked.

Abbey nodded. “I just want everything back the way it was before he left.”

“So what’s the problem?”

“He said there are changes that need to be made.” Abbey pouted.

“What kind of changes?”

"For starters, he wants me to get a job."

And the only job Abbey had ever wanted was to be a wife and mother—and Molly suspected it was the unrealized latter part of that desire that was the cause of most of her sister's marital problems.

"It's not that I'm opposed to working," Abbey said. "I've just never been really good at anything."

"You've never *tried* to be good at anything," Molly corrected. "Except shopping."

Her sister brightened at that. "I could get a job as a personal shopper."

"At least then you'd be spending other people's money."

"Do you really think I'm qualified?"

"I have no doubt you're qualified, but I'm not sure there's much demand for personal shoppers outside the big cities."

Abbey sighed. "You're probably right."

Another few minutes passed, during which Molly tried to discard the thought that popped into her mind, but it refused to go away until finally, with more resignation than enthusiasm, she said, "You could work here."

Abbey stared at her as if she'd suggested that she dance naked on the tables instead of serve meals to the customers seated at them.

"Work?" she echoed. "Here?"

"I know it's an odd concept, but there are several of us who actually do so. The pay's not great," Molly admitted. "But the tips are pretty good." And after the abrupt and unexpected departure of one of her waitresses, Molly was desperate for another pair of hands to work the dinner shift. She'd been doing everything she could to help out herself, but she was already feeling the effects of the extra hours on her feet, and knew that couldn't continue.

"Tips?"

"Of course, you'd have to learn to smile instead of scowl if you wanted to earn any."

Abbey sighed. "When can I start?"

"Four o'clock."

Molly wasn't surprised that Abbey showed up less than five minutes before her shift was scheduled to begin, but she was pleased that her sister apparently remembered the routine from when she'd waited tables through high school. Abbey caught on to the routine quickly and managed to take orders and deliver meals with little mishap. She finished her first shift with sore feet and a pocketful of tips that, when added up, elicited a weary smile.

Abbey worked again the next afternoon, and the day after that, and by the end of the week, Molly was actually starting to think the arrangement might work out.

Though there hadn't been an empty table during the midday rush, the restaurant was now mostly empty and Molly poured herself a cup of decaf and took a seat at the bar. There was a table with three men in suits who were finishing up a business meeting along with their lunches, another at which was seated a couple of older women who seemed more interested in conversation than their meals, and at a booth in the back, a young couple lingering over coffee.

Molly was proud that her business appealed to such an eclectic group, and pleased that the additional funds she'd spent on advertising over the past twelve months was proving to be a good investment. Shea's had once been "the little roadside bar just past the sharp curve in the highway," now it was "that fabulous little restaurant just past the sharp curve in the highway."

She hadn't taken the first sip of her coffee when her brother-in-law came in.

"If you're looking for your wife, she just left."

"I'm not," Jason said, then walked behind the bar, poured himself a cup of coffee and sat down beside her.

It was the first time she'd seen him in the restaurant since he and Abbey separated a few months earlier, and she was as curious as she was wary about his reasons for being here now. Because he, too, didn't seem to think there was anything wrong with dumping his problems in Molly's lap, despite having dumped her to marry her sister.

"I have a business proposition to discuss with you."

Now she was *really* curious, but she just sipped her decaf and waited for him to explain.

Instead of speaking, he set a cashier's check beside her cup.

Her eyes popped open wide as she took in the numbers.

"Where did you get that kind of cash?"

"My severance package from Raycroft Industries."

She'd read about the proposed merger of the local manufacturing plant with a multinational corporation several months earlier and had wondered how it might affect her brother-in-law, who had worked there for the past half-dozen years.

"I'd like to buy into a partnership," he said.

For the amount of the check he was offering, he could buy the whole restaurant, and Molly was almost tempted to let him do so. She'd certainly feel more comfortable selling out than going into partnership with a man who had betrayed her once already. "Why?" she asked instead.

"I have managerial experience and I think I'd enjoy working here—and working with Abbey might give both of us something to focus on other than the baby she wants so badly and can't have."

Which led Molly to suspect that Abbey had decided she'd rather own the restaurant than simply work in it—and, like everything else she'd ever wanted, there was a man willing to give it to her.

"Is this what Abbey wants?" she asked him.

"If she had her way, we'd spend the whole amount on fertility treatments. But I think she could be convinced to agree to this."

Molly felt an instinctive tug of sympathy for what her sister and brother-in-law had been through, and a twinge of guilt that what they'd struggled for so desperately had happened so easily for her. And then a surge of annoyance at letting herself experience even that momentary twinge when it was Abbey and Jason together who had destroyed her own dreams.

"Have you really thought about this, or is it an impulse?"

"You know I don't do anything on impulse," Jason said.

"Weddings in Las Vegas aside?"

"It was one wedding, and it was because Abbey and I didn't know how to tell you that we'd fallen in love."

Molly sighed, because she knew it was true and because—nine years later—she was over it, or at least she felt that she should be. Was it the depth of the hurt that made her heart still ache? Or was it something lacking inside herself that made her unable to truly forgive their betrayal?

In either case, she knew it was time she got over her resentment and got on with her life, and maybe Jason was offering her the chance to finally do just that.

"Speaking of weddings," she said, "I'm going to Tesoro del Mar for Fiona and Scott's."

Although Abbey was the bride's cousin, too, she'd never been as close to Fiona as Molly was. And Fiona had never forgiven her for stealing Molly's fiancé, holding so tightly to her grudge against Abbey that she hadn't even wanted to invite her youngest cousin to the wedding. It was their grandmother who had insisted that she do the right thing, and while Abbey and Jason would be invited to attend the rescheduled reception in a few months, Fiona refused to extend the close circle who had been invited to the island ceremony to include them.

"I was going to ask Karen and Sam to cover my night shifts," Molly continued, "but if you wanted to take them instead, it would give you a chance to see if this is what you really want, before making a final decision."

He reached for her hand as she pushed her stool back. "Thanks, Molly. I know you don't owe me anything, but I appreciate this opportunity."

"Don't screw it up."

"I won't," he promised.

When Eric walked into Shea's, he saw Molly holding hands with another man and felt the churn of dark and unfamiliar emotions in his belly. He had no claim to her. One night of sex, no matter how spectacular, gave him no proprietary right, but that knowledge didn't negate the fact that when he'd seen the other man reach for her, he'd felt his own hands curl into fists and heard only one thought in his mind—*mine.*

She was on her way to the door when she saw him a minute later. She smiled easily, as if she hadn't just been cozied up with some other guy.

"You're a little late for lunch today, aren't you?" she asked him.

"I had lunch with Fiona and Scott today," he told her, responding in a similarly casual tone.

"And you're early for dinner," she prompted.

He managed to smile. "I actually came to see you, if you've got a few minutes."

"Can we take those minutes upstairs? I've been here since eight and I want a change of scenery and popcorn." She started up to her apartment without waiting to see if he agreed.

He followed.

She unlocked the door, kicked off her shoes and moved into the kitchen. Snagging a box of Orville Redenbacher's from the cupboard, she unwrapped the cellophane from a package and pressed a couple of buttons on the microwave.

He frowned, remembering what she'd said about having been at the restaurant since eight. "That isn't your lunch, is it?"

"Not really. I snacked on some cheese balls and potato skins in the kitchen, but I was suddenly craving popcorn." She frowned at that.

"Vegetables are one of the food groups, too," he pointed out.

The popcorn had mostly stopped popping, and she smiled as she opened the door of the microwave and pulled the bag out. "And corn is a vegetable."

She tore open the top of the bag and a puff of steam and rich, buttery scent escaped. "Why did you want to see me?"

"You mean, other than the fact that I really like looking at you?" he couldn't help but tease, and had the pleasure of watching her cheeks flush.

"Other than that," she agreed dryly.

"I wanted to let you know that I finalized the travel arrangements. Scott and Fiona are coming with me tomorrow, but you can fly in with Scott's parents next Wednesday, if that works better for you."

"My grandparents aren't coming at all?" she asked.

He shook his head. "Fiona didn't seem surprised."

"I'm not really, either," she admitted. "I was just hoping… Neither of us have our parents anymore. My mom walked out, my dad died, and Fiona's mom and dad were both killed in a car accident a few years back, so aside from each other and Abbey, our grandparents are the only real family we have."

"Do you want me to talk to them, see if I could change their minds?"

She smiled. "Thanks, but no one changes my grandmother's mind about anything once she's made it up and she refuses to go anywhere near an airplane."

"So do you want to come tomorrow or next week?" Eric asked her.

She hesitated, then said, "I think tomorrow could work."

He was both pleased and surprised by her response. "I thought you didn't want to be away from the restaurant for too long."

"I didn't," she admitted. "But I had an interesting conversation with someone before you showed up and I'm starting to think that this is something I have to do."

"An interesting conversation with the guy at the bar?" He shouldn't have asked—he knew it was none of his business. But the question had been eating away at him since he'd seen them together, noted the obvious familiarity in their interactions with one another.

"Jason," she said, and nodded.

"And who is Jason?"

"My ex-fiancé."

He scowled. "You were engaged to that guy?"

"A long time ago," she said.

Which made him feel marginally better until he remembered that the guy had been holding her hand not such a long time ago.

"What time tomorrow?" she asked, in what seemed to him an obvious attempt to change the topic but might simply have been a desire to know the specifics of their travel plans.

"Six-thirty," he told her.

"A.M.?"

"Yeah."

Molly crumpled up the now empty popcorn bag and tossed it into the garbage. "Then I'm going to kick you out now so I can pack because I have to be back downstairs in an hour."

As usual, Molly worked until closing that night. Jason came in at ten and stayed behind the bar with his sister-in-law, shadowing her every movement. Usually Molly could close everything up and be cashed out within half an hour of locking the door behind the last customer, but having to explain every step to Jason meant the routine took more than twice as long.

Still, she was awake and ready when the knock came at the door at precisely 6:30 a.m. the next morning—if not exactly alert.

She was surprised that Eric had come up instead of sending his driver, and more than a little disconcerted when he swore softly in Spanish and reached out to her.

"Mi Dios." He brushed a thumb gently beneath her eye, tracing the purple shadows she hadn't even tried to cover with make-up. "You don't look as if you've slept."

"I got a few hours," she said, shifting away, as much from the casual intimacy of the gesture as the surge of warmth evoked by his tender touch, to reach for her suitcase.

He immediately pried the handle from her fingers. "I've got it."

She lifted a brow. "You take control quite easily for a man who's probably had servants picking up after him his whole life."

"No one waits on anyone else in the navy, regardless of title or rank," he told her.

The statement reminded her not just that he'd served his country but of the scars on his body that had been earned in that service. But instead of thinking of the injury that had ended his career, she found herself thinking of his taut, hard muscles and warm, smooth skin and the heat of his body moving against hers. Just the memories were enough to make her body tingle all over, stirring up yearnings that had been long dormant until the first night he'd walked into the bar.

Over the past several weeks, she'd managed—with effort—to keep those memories at bay. Mostly, anyway. But her tired brain was no match for the rising heat in her blood evoked by his nearness. She'd read about the enhanced sensual awareness that many women experienced during pregnancy and knew that she was one of them.

"Damn hormones," she muttered under her breath.

He turned. "Did you say something?"

She just shook her head and followed him down the stairs.

While Scott and Fiona were cuddled close together, talking about the wedding or the future or whatever else soon-to-be-marrieds talked about, Eric watched Molly sleep.

He'd watched her sleep the night they'd spent together in her bed, when exhaustion had finally overwhelmed the passion that brought them together. He wanted her now as much as he'd wanted her then. The only thing that had prevented him from waking her and slipping into the wet heat of her sexy little body was the realization that they'd depleted the store of condoms he'd bought from the vending machine in the men's room.

As he watched her now, he wondered what it was about this one woman that had taken hold of him. And he was baffled that the woman who had once been so warm and willing in his arms was so determined to keep him at arm's length now.

He knew his reappearance in her life had thrown her for a loop, but he suspected that there was more going on than that. It was as if, in the few weeks that he'd been gone, her entire life had been turned upside down. He wasn't egotistical enough to believe that he was responsible for that. As spectacular as their night together had been, neither of them had expected it would be any more than that.

But he got the impression there was something going on in her life that weighed on her mind, that was responsible for the shadows beneath her eyes and the wariness in her gaze. Or maybe he was making a big deal out of nothing. Maybe her exhaustion was simply the result of having been up too late last night and needing to be up again early this morning. Knowing the hours that she worked, he was glad she'd managed to shut down and rest for a few hours during their journey.

He was also glad she'd agreed to come to Tesoro del Mar in advance of the wedding. Not that there was a lot of planning to do—the palace staff would take care of most of the details without blinking an eye, as they'd done for the prince regent's wedding six years earlier and the celebration of Marcus's nuptials three years after that.

One of the perks of being a royal, as Marcus liked to say, was having staff to whom to delegate. Ironic, considering that Marcus had met his wife while traveling in the United States under their mother's maiden name so as to keep his royal status hidden, and had spent several months having tasks—such as mucking out stalls at his wife's Thoroughbred training facility—delegated to him. Of course, she hadn't been his wife at the time, and she hadn't been thrilled to learn the true identity of her stable hand, but once again, their feelings for one another had proven stronger than any of the obstacles between them—one of which had been the accident that ended Eric's naval career.

He felt a twinge in his hip and shifted in his seat. A phantom pain was brought on by even the most fleeting flashback of the moment that had changed his life. He was getting more adept at pushing the memories—and the accompanying panic—aside. He did so now, focusing his thoughts again on his friend's imminent wedding.

No one outside of the family had ever been married at the palace, but Rowan and Marcus had both agreed that Scott was part of their family even if it wasn't Santiago blood in his veins.

After Marcus and Jewel married, there had been a lot of speculation throughout the media that Eric would be next—which he had to agree was likely since he was the last unmarried Santiago brother and his oldest nephew was still just a teenager. And he certainly had no philosophical or personal objections to marriage—he'd just never met a woman who made him think in terms of forever. He'd never even met a woman who lingered in his mind after he'd left her bed...until Molly.

He turned away from the window to confirm that she was still sleeping. She was, and in sleep, her worries seemed to finally—if only temporarily—be forgotten. Her features were relaxed, the dark fan of her lashes casting a shadow against her pale cheek. He knew her skin was soft, and smoother even than the finest silk. And hidden beneath her lashes were eyes of the most startling and vivid shade of blue, eyes that had darkened and clouded in the throes of passion, the color shifting and changing not unlike the moods of a turbulent sea.

Mi Dios, he was getting turned on just by watching her sleep. Watching her sleep and remembering, and remembering—wanting.

Sexual frustration was a new—and not at all pleasant—experience for him. In the past, whenever he'd wanted the companionship of a woman, it had been easy enough to come by. But after the accident he'd turned his attention to rehabilitation. He'd been so intensely focused on healing his body that he hadn't allowed anything to distract him from the task. Not until the night he'd walked into Shea's Bar & Grill and spotted Molly working the tap.

Almost three years of abstinence seemed a reasonable explanation for the extent of his reaction to her, and his response to the experience of making love with her. Afterward, he managed to convince himself that the sex hadn't really been as spectacular as he remembered, that it was just so long since he'd had sex that the experience only seemed heightened.

And yet, back in Tesoro del Mar, where the women were plentiful and beautiful and willing, there hadn't been one who had tempted him into her bed. Not one who tempted him to forget about Molly.

She shifted, her head rolling from one side to the other. She hadn't reclined her seat—probably because she hadn't intended to fall asleep, but exhaustion had won out. A slight furrow creased her brow as she shifted again, still asleep but obviously not very comfortable. She drew up one knee and leaned back so that her head fell against his shoulder.

Her hair tickled his cheek, the scent of her shampoo teased his nostrils, and he held his breath while he waited for her to wake. She didn't, but snuggled in, apparently finding a position that was finally comfortable—at least for her. Because while he didn't mind having her close, he was suddenly uncomfortably aware of her nearness, her softness, her femininity—and *everything* that was male within him responded.

He glanced over at Scott and Fiona, saw that they were still cuddled close together, talking quietly, so he just shifted his seat back and settled in, while Molly's scent—and his desire—continued to torment him.

Chapter Six

Molly woke just as the wheels touched down on land. But even when she felt the plane make contact with the runway, it took a moment for that fact to penetrate her consciousness. She'd been so tired lately—physically and mentally exhausted. Even when she slept, her sleep had been restless, unsettled. But this time, she awoke feeling rested and refreshed—at least until she realized that she'd been using Eric as a pillow.

She jolted upright, her face flaming. "I…um…sorry," was the best apology she could manage to stammer out.

His smile was slow, easy. "No need to be embarrassed," he said, speaking softly so that Scott and Fiona, seated across from them, wouldn't hear his words. "After all, it isn't the first time you've fallen asleep in my arms."

"But it will be the last," she muttered in response.

"Your choice, of course," he assured her, unbuckling his seat belt.

Molly fumbled with hers, unfamiliar with the mechanism.

Eric watched her struggle for a moment before reaching over to release the clasp.

She held her breath as the backs of his knuckles brushed against her middle. Through the soft cotton of her T-shirt, her stomach quivered in response to the brief contact that reminded her not just of the baby that was nestled deep in her womb, but that it was *his* baby.

And in that moment, she really wanted to tell him. She wanted to share the joy and excitement of every minute of her pregnancy with him. But aside from the fact that an airplane probably wasn't the most appropriate place to share the news, especially with their friends seated across from them, there was the fear that he might not share her joy and excitement.

And if his reception of the news was less than enthusiastic, she shouldn't be surprised. Even she'd been more shocked than pleased when Dr. Morgan had advised her of the pregnancy, and though she already loved her baby more than she would ever have thought was possible, she knew she couldn't expect that Eric would feel the same. Which was why she knew it was important to choose the right time and place—and then to give him time and space to absorb the news and consider all of the implications.

No, it was definitely not the-airplane-has-just-landed-and-he's-so-close-that-I-can't-even-think-straight-because-my-hormones-are-running-riot kind of news.

Instead, she only said, "Thank you."

He released the ends of her seat belt. "You're welcome."

The warmth of his breath caressed her cheek, and a wave of heat washed over her, leaving her weak and flushed.

It was as if every nerve ending in her body was attuned to him, sending tingles of awareness and wanting through her system every time he even glanced in her direction. She'd never responded to anyone as she responded to him.

She wanted to blame it on the pregnancy, all those hormones running amok through her system, but she knew it was Eric.

Because the fact was, she wouldn't *be* pregnant if she hadn't had the same instinctive response to him from the very beginning.

The limo driver took them along the coast, so that they were flanked by rolling green hills on one side and powdery sand and crystal blue waters on the other. It was all so peaceful now, but Molly imagined that could change in the blink of an eye, that a storm could churn up the water so that the waves lashed against the rocks like angry sea monsters.

A fanciful thought, she knew, encouraged by the inherent beauty and mystery of this land that could make her imagination run as wild as it had when she was a child. Or maybe it wasn't so surprising that she was remembering childhood dreams—after all, she was riding with a prince on the way to his castle. She just had to remember that this wasn't a magical enchantment and she wasn't looking for a "happily ever after" ending.

Still, there were thoughts and ideas swirling through her mind that she vowed to jot down at the earliest opportunity. And when she caught her first glimpse of the royal palace, she couldn't entirely stifle her gasp of surprised pleasure.

It stood high atop a jutting cliff, a stunning structure of towers and turrets that was both more imposing and impressive than she could have imagined. She'd been curious enough to do some reading about the Santiago family and knew they had ruled long and ruled well, and she sensed that this castle, standing strong and proud on the hill, wasn't just a symbol to the people of Tesoro del Mar but a promise.

Another fanciful thought, perhaps, and while she'd been prepared for a fairy tale—something reminiscent of a little girl's misty-edged dreams—the reality was somehow even better.

The driver parked at the bottom of a set of wide stone steps that led up to a pair of imposing wooden doors that looked as if they could withstand the attack of a medieval battering ram. Those massive doors opened into an entranceway that was bigger than Molly's entire apartment, with a floor made of marble and walls papered in something that added hints of both shimmer and depth. Sun streamed through the tall arched windows that bracketed the doors, bathing the space in warmth and light, and fresh flowers spilled out of tall vases so that the air was perfumed with their fragrant scent.

They were greeted by a housekeeper who curtsied to the prince before advising that the guests' rooms were ready. Eric thanked and assured her that he would show them the way, then directed them up the curving stairs to the second floor, then the third. He guided them down a wide hallway, where the sound of their steps was muffled by the plush carpet. The walls were hung with pictures and tapestries, and the windows draped with velvet curtains.

Fiona and Scott were delivered to their suite before Eric led Molly a little bit farther down the hall.

"Your rooms overlook the gardens," he told her.

Not a room but *rooms,* she noted, as he opened an ornately carved door and led her into a sitting room that boasted a couple of richly upholstered chairs on either side of a stone fireplace and an antique writing desk and balloon-back chair. Behind the desk was a window, wide and multipaned, with the promised view of gardens that boasted a stunning array of vibrant colors and exotic scents.

Through the sitting room was the bedroom with a tall chest of drawers and matching bedside table of gleaming cherrywood and a wide bed topped with a thick duvet and piled with fluffy pillows. The bathroom was half the size of the bedroom again, with a deep whirlpool tub and separate shower, toilet and pedestal sink.

"If you need anything, you only need to ring for housekeeping," he told her, gesturing to the phone beside the bed.

"You might need a crowbar to pry me out of here after the wedding," she warned.

"Then maybe you'll decide to stay," he said, sounding as if he meant it.

"You know I can't," she told him.

But there was a part of her that already wished she could.

Eric had decided to give Molly space.

As much as he was eager to spend time with her and anxious to show off his homeland, he had sensed a new wariness in her since they'd landed in Tesoro del Mar—as if she knew that he now had the home turf advantage and was waiting to see how he would use it. He decided it couldn't hurt to let her wait—and wonder—a little while longer.

It was Fiona who gave him the opportunity, and the opening, he'd been hoping for. Saturday morning, only their third full day on the island, he found her alone by the pool.

"Lose your fiancé already?" he teased.

"He went down to the stables to take a ride with Rowan and Christian."

"What about Molly?" he asked, with what he thought was casual interest.

"She should be down shortly." But she frowned when she said it.

"You're supposed to be relaxing not worrying," Eric told her, lowering himself onto the edge of the vacant lounger beside hers. "I assure you, all the wedding details are being taken care of."

"I'm not worrying about the wedding," she said.

"But you're worried about something."

She sighed. "Molly."

"Is something wrong?"

"I don't know," she admitted. "I know she argued with her sister before we left Texas, although that's not really unusual. And even before that—for the past several weeks now—she's seemed really distracted. As if she's worried about something but she won't tell me what it is."

"She probably figures you have enough on your mind right now."

"She used to tell me everything," Fiona said. "I don't have any siblings, and although Molly does, we've always been as close as sisters. Closer than Molly and Abbey, that's for sure, especially after the stunt Abbey pulled with Jason."

"Molly's ex-fiancé?"

"How did you know they were engaged?" she asked curiously.

"I saw them talking at the restaurant one day, and she told me."

"That's not usually something she talks about," Fiona mused.

"Bad break-up?" he wondered aloud.

"Obviously she didn't tell you everything."

"What more is there?"

"The fact that he's now Abbey's husband."

"Molly's sister married Molly's former fiancé?"

"He was still current when Abbey seduced him." Fiona winced. "I can't believe I told you that. But I figured if you'd met Jason, you knew he was Abbey's husband."

No, Molly had conveniently neglected to mention that fact, and it didn't take a genius to figure out why. He'd asked about the guy he saw her with. She'd used his status as an ex to remind Eric that she wasn't his—a lightweight reminder if he knew that the ex was married to someone else.

"I know it sounds like something out of a soap opera, but that's exactly what happened. And though Molly keeps insisting that she's over him, I wonder if a person can ever get over that kind of betrayal. I worry that she won't ever open up her heart to anyone else."

"That's not something you can make happen," he told her, knowing—and regretting—that it was true.

"I know," she admitted. "It's just that she's my best friend, and while no one else might have noticed the change, I've seen it. She still smiles and laughs and even dates occasionally, but she's so guarded now, so careful not to get too close to anyone.

"I'd hoped that coming here would be good for her. She needed a change of scenery, a change of pace, but she's been so preoccupied lately, obviously worried about something."

"Give her some time," he suggested. "It's only day three."

"I know." She picked up her bottle of sunscreen, reapplied the lotion to her shoulders and arms. "And you've already done so much—none of this would be possible without you and I know I won't ever be able to repay you, but I really want to ask you for another favor."

"What's that?"

"Would you—if you had some free time—mind showing Molly around the island? It might take her mind off whatever is bothering her."

And Eric realized there were times when opportunity didn't just knock, it threw open the door and tossed out a welcome mat.

"I wouldn't mind at all," he said.

Despite his claim that he wanted to spend time with her when they were on the island, Molly hadn't seen a lot of Eric since they'd arrived in Tesoro del Mar. Though she tried not to dwell on the fact of his title, he was a prince and, as such, obviously had royal duties to fulfill. What those duties were she couldn't even begin to guess, but obviously they took up a lot of his time.

Not that she'd left her own responsibilities behind. She called the restaurant daily for an update, usually talking to Karen rather than Jason because Karen had been at Shea's a long time. Molly trusted that she would tell her if there were any problems with the nighttime shifts. So far, everything was running smoothly, which should have reassured Molly but somehow made her feel extraneous instead—and left her with far too much time to think about Eric.

Aside from being wildly attracted to him, during the past couple of weeks in Texas, she'd actually started to like him and enjoy spending time with him—or she would if she could only forget he was a prince.

Since landing in Tesoro del Mar, she hadn't been able to forget that for a minute.

Upon their arrival at the palace, he'd been bowed and curtsied to more times than she could count. He didn't seem to demand or even expect such deference, but he accepted it. As the second oldest son—no, he was the third born, she remembered now. Fiona had briefed her on the history of the royal family, including the tragic story of how Prince Julian—who had ruled the country prior to Rowan becoming prince regent—and his wife, Princess Catherine, had been killed by a freak explosion on their yacht. As a result, Prince Rowan had inherited not only the throne but custody of his older brother's three children.

He seemed to have adapted to sudden parenthood well, as evidenced by the close bond he shared with Christian, Lexi and Damon, as well as his two children with Lara—the former royal nanny.

Matthew and William were two of the most adorable kids Molly had ever seen. When introduced to Rowan and Lara's children, her first thought had been that they both bore a strong resemblance to their uncle Eric. Then she met Rowan and realized the dark hair and eyes and strong bone structure weren't specific to Eric but were family traits.

In fact, she nearly did a double take the first time she saw the prince regent, which prompted Scott to say, "Marcus and Eric look even more alike. When we were kids, people were constantly getting the two of them confused—which we learned to exploit whenever possible."

Eric had smiled at that. "Remember when the gardener swore he'd seen me running through his freshly planted flowerbeds and Nanny Adele argued, just as vehemently, that I'd been in the pool with you when it happened?"

"Marcus was the one who raced through the dirt," Molly guessed.

"No, it was Eric," Scott admitted now. "But seeing Marcus in the pool—conveniently wearing Eric's bathing suit to confuse everyone further—made the gardener question his conviction, which meant that Prince Eduardo couldn't be sure who should be punished."

"So you got away with trampling the flowers?" she asked Eric.

He shook his head. "No—we all got punished. My father was a big believer in taking responsibility for one's actions, and he personally supervised while Marcus and I replanted the whole garden. And he made Scott water the flowers, because he was an accessory."

She'd smiled as she'd listened to their retelling of the story, amused by their boyhood antics and pleased to hear the respect and affection in his voice when he talked about his father, confident that he would want to develop that same solid relationship with his own child.

But she still didn't know how he would react to the news that he was going to be a father himself, and she still hadn't figured out how to share that news when the wedding was finally over.

Right now, however, she was more concerned about what she was going to wear for dinner with Fiona and Scott and Eric because tonight, for the first time since the night of their arrival of the palace, he was free of whatever obligations had kept him occupied and was taking them all out.

She was scanning the meager contents of her closet when her cousin slipped into her room. Fiona held up the dress she was carrying so that Molly could appreciate the simple sheath style in a silky fabric that was somewhere between blue and green and absolutely stunning.

"How did you know I'd have nothing to wear?"

"Because I know you and you wouldn't have thought to pack much beyond your bridesmaid dress, a bathing suit and a toothbrush."

"I thought *you* were bringing the bridesmaid dress."

Fiona's face actually paled. "You didn't—"

"Kidding," Molly interrupted, and grinned.

Her cousin huffed out a breath. "Not funny."

"It was funny," she countered. "It just wasn't very nice, so I'll apologize and say 'thank you'—not just for knowing me so well but for having excellent taste and wearing the same dress size I do."

"*And* the same shoe size," Fiona said, holding out a pair of low-heeled sandals to go with the dress.

"Thanks," Molly said again.

"You can thank me by putting it on—I'm dying to see it on you."

So Molly stripped out of her robe and slipped into the dress, sighing as the silky fabric floated over her body. "I might not ever give this back."

Fiona sighed. "I don't think I'm going to want it back—it looks so much better on you than it ever did on me."

Molly knew that couldn't be true—she'd never seen her cousin look anything less than stunning—but she appreciated the compliment.

Fiona settled back on the bed and they chatted casually while

Molly finished getting ready. She didn't know if they would be dining inside or out and she didn't want her hair tangling around her face if it was windy, so she fashioned a quick French twist and secured it with a handful of pins.

"Does it work?" she asked, turning to her cousin for approval.

"It works," Fiona agreed. "In fact, it looks fabulous."

"And you look a little underdressed," she suddenly realized.

Fiona looked down at the cover-up she wore over her bikini and smiled as she slid off the bed, already making her way toward the door. "Actually, I'm dressed exactly right for a romantic picnic on the beach."

"We're having a picnic on the beach?"

Her cousin shook her head. "Scott and I are having a picnic. *You're* going out for dinner with Eric."

"Fiona…"

It was all she managed before her cousin slipped out the door, closing it firmly between them.

Chapter Seven

Molly stared at the back of the door for a long minute, considering her options. She knew she'd been set up and even knowing her cousin had the best of intentions, she didn't appreciate it. She was tempted to refuse to go out, just to prove that she wouldn't be manipulated, but that seemed both petty and spiteful and she wasn't, as a rule, either of those things. At the moment, however, she was apprehensive about spending time with Eric.

Her nervousness escalated when she left her room and found him waiting for her at the bottom of the stairs.

She felt her cheeks flush as his gaze skimmed over her, from the top of her head to the tips of her toes and everywhere in between. She trailed a hand down the smoothly polished banister, grateful for its solid support as she descended toward him. When she neared the bottom step, he offered her his hand, and she took it.

"You look…incredible."

"Thank you, Your Highness." Then she curtsied, because it

seemed appropriate. "You look quite like Prince Charming yourself."

"Prince Charming, huh? That's quite a reputation to live up to."

"I have no doubt you'll manage."

He smiled, and the slow, sensual curve of his lips made her pulse leap.

She knew how those lips tasted—their tangy masculine flavor. And she knew how they felt—nibbling her throat, nuzzling her breasts, skimming over her heated skin. Talk about heat—just the memories of the night they'd spent together had her temperature climbing toward the roof.

"I'll do my best," he said, leading her to the door beyond which he promised, "Your chariot awaits."

Her chariot was actually a sleek and sexy sports car unlike anything she had ever seen before.

"It's a Saleen S7 Twin Turbo," he told her, as if that was supposed to mean anything to a woman who drove a perfectly nice but unexceptional Saturn. "It has a seven-hundred-and-fifty horsepower V8 engine and can go from zero to sixty in less than three seconds."

"We're not going to do that, are we?" she asked, more than a little apprehensively.

He chuckled. "No. And it's not actually mine—it belongs to my brother Marcus. He was always into fast cars and fast women—before he met Jewel, anyway. Besides being an attention-getter, it's a heck of a lot of fun to drive."

And it was, she found, fun to ride in.

Maybe he didn't take it from zero to sixty in less than three seconds, but he did go fast, zipping through the streets such that everything was a blur through the window.

He drove into the town of Port Augustine, a seaside village bustling with tourists and commerce. As he navigated his way through the city streets, he proved to be a fabulous tour guide, knowledgeable about the island's history and geography.

He parked in a public lot, but it was only when he donned the baseball cap and mirrored sunglasses that she remembered he was a prince and that this was his country and the disguise—lame though it was—was probably necessary if he didn't want to be recognized.

"Ashamed to be seen with me?" she asked, only half joking. Because while she was confident that she looked her best in her borrowed dress, she didn't doubt that a prince was used to escorting much more beautiful and glamorous women than she would ever be.

"On the contrary," he said. "I am always pleased to have the company of a gorgeous woman. But if you are seen with me, I'm afraid you may be hounded by the local paparazzi for the rest of your stay in Tesoro del Mar."

"So the disguise is for my benefit?" she asked skeptically.

"And mine," he admitted. "Because I don't want to share a single minute of the time we have together with anyone else."

"If you wanted to blend in, you might have chosen a less conspicuous vehicle," she pointed out.

"But I wanted to impress you, too."

She couldn't help but smile at that.

"Do I look like an American tourist?" he asked her now.

She noted the Texas Rangers logo on the cap and figured it had been a gift from Scott—or perhaps he'd just borrowed it from his friend. But if his intention was to blend in, she didn't think he would ever manage that. Even with the hat pushed down over his thick, dark hair and those deep, compelling eyes covered with the reflective lenses, he wasn't a man who could walk around without attracting attention. He was too tall, too compelling and far too sexy for Molly's peace of mind. Not that she intended to admit any of those thoughts to the prince.

"Maybe from a distance," she said. "And only so long as you don't say anything, because no one hearing you speak would ever mistake you for a Texan."

"I'll let you do all the talking," he promised, slinging a companionable arm across her shoulders.

"My high school Spanish is more than a little rusty," she warned.

"Everyone here speaks English. Though Tesoro del Mar is officially a bilingual country—with Spanish and French as its two official languages—English is just as common and is taught in all of the schools."

He was proud of his homeland, she could hear it in his voice when he talked about the country and its people. He was a man who would have felt it was an honor and a privilege to serve in the navy, to do his part to keep his country safe, and she could only imagine how devastated he'd been to have that opportunity taken away.

The more she got to know him, the more facets she saw. He was a prince, a soldier, a hero. But mostly he was a good man, a man her baby would be proud to know was its father.

They walked along the streets of Port Augustine, browsed in the shops, drank espresso at an outdoor café, then walked some more before returning to the car.

"Getting hungry yet?" Eric asked as he drove toward the north coast.

"I am," she admitted. "I didn't think I'd want to eat for a week after the lunch Fiona and I had by the pool, but all that walking changed my mind."

"All part of my plan," he told her, "so that you can fully appreciate the experience of Tradewinds Ristorante. I promise you, Genevieve is a culinary genius."

"You must be a frequent customer if you're on a first-name basis with the chef."

"She used to work at the palace," he explained. "Her father still does. In fact, Marcel is the one who put together the sample menu for Fiona and Scott's wedding."

"So why did his daughter leave?"

"She wanted to succeed on the basis of her own work, build her own reputation."

"Obviously she has," Molly said, noting that the line of customers waiting to be seated extended outside of the door. "Do you have a reservation?"

"Please," he chided. "My title is all the reservation I need."

"I thought you were incognito today."

"Not while my stomach is rumbling." But instead of leading her to the front of the line, he guided her around to the back of the building and through an unmarked door.

She recognized the sounds of a busy kitchen—the clang of pots being shifted from prep area to burner to service counter, the rhythmic thunk of a blade chopping and dicing, the whir of a blender pulverizing. And the scents—mmm…the air was rich with flavors that were tangy and spicy and tart and sweet.

"What are you doing with that?" A woman's voice rang with authority through the din, silencing all other murmurs of conversation.

The junior cook to whom the question had been directed flinched as he turned to face his boss's wrath. "I was adding the béarnaise sauce."

"Those potatoes are charred," she pointed out in a cool voice, lifting the plate from the counter to inspect the offending spuds more closely. "And if you thought you could cover that up with the sauce, you were wrong."

"But the order is for Prince Cameron and he does not like to be kept waiting."

"He would like it even less if something came out of this

kitchen that was not prepared to my exacting specifications." And with that, she dumped the contents of the plate into the garbage.

The young apprentice flushed. "Of course, Mademoiselle."

"You will apologize to His Highness for the wait and offer a round of complimentary drinks to his table while I prepare his meal properly."

This directive was met with a brief nod before he hurried out of the kitchen to do his boss's bidding, while the dark-haired woman set to work, muttering under her breath in French.

"The only thing missing is the crack of a whip," Eric commented, loudly enough to ensure that he would be heard.

The tiny chef spun around, her brows drawn together in a scowl that immediately smoothed out when she identified the speaker. "Your Highness," she said, her lips curving into a wide smile.

The words and quick curtsy might have been formal, the embrace they shared after was not. Eric kissed both of the woman's cheeks, as Molly had learned was the European fashion, though with more enthusiasm than she thought was typical.

When he drew back, the chef's cheeks were flushed—whether from the heat of the kitchen or the pleasure of Eric's attention—Molly didn't want to guess.

"There must be a full moon tonight—the royals are all coming out of the woodwork," she teased.

"Please do not place me in the same category as my cousin."

"My apologies, Your Highness."

Her apology sounded more teasing than contrite and, judging from the way Eric's eyes narrowed, he knew it. But he only drew Molly forward. "Genevieve, I'd like you to meet Molly Shea. Molly, this is the incomparable Mademoiselle Fleury, chef *extraordinaire* and proprietor of Tradewinds."

Molly shook the proffered hand, and though the other

woman's smile was warm, she sensed that she was being as carefully measured as the ingredients for a soufflé.

"It's always a pleasure to meet a friend of a friend," Genevieve said.

"Likewise," Molly murmured.

She felt Eric's hand on her waist, his fingers curling over her hip. "Do you have a table for us?" he asked.

Genevieve rolled her eyes and turned to Molly. "He comes in at seven o'clock on a Saturday night and expects that I will have a table?"

Molly shrugged apologetically.

The chef shook her head. "You take too much for granted, Your Highness."

"Because I know you would never disappoint me," Eric said.

Genevieve sighed. "Paolo will make up the table on the balcony, so that you can have some privacy."

He smiled and kissed both of her cheeks again. *"Merci, mon ami."*

"C'est toujours mon plaisir."

A few minutes later, Molly and Eric were escorted up a carved stone staircase. The restaurant was in a prime location overlooking the sparkling turquoise waters of the Mediterranean. The atmosphere on Genevieve's private balcony was enhanced by the soft music floating up from the dining room below and the scents of jasmine and vanilla emanating from the pots of flowers set around the ledge.

The table was covered with a neatly pressed linen cloth that was as blue as the sea; the crystal sparkled and the silver gleamed in the flickering light of a trio of candles.

Molly couldn't help but be impressed by the hastily assembled scene—and a little wary about the romantic ambience. They were casual acquaintances who had been one-time lovers and she hoped, for the sake of their child, that they might develop a friendship of sorts, but she wasn't looking for anything more than that.

There was no doubt, however, that this scene had been set for romance, and it made her wonder how many other women he had brought here—how many dates he'd impressed with a replica of this very same setting. It shouldn't matter; she told herself it didn't matter. This—whatever this was between them—wasn't a date.

But she couldn't help but ask, "Come here often?"

"I enjoy my privacy as much as a good meal, and Genevieve is kind enough to accommodate me in both respects."

"And is obviously discreet enough not to blink when you introduce her to your…friends."

He grinned. "I do trust Genevieve. I wouldn't have brought you here otherwise. But if you think this is part of my usual seduction routine, you'd be wrong. Because the truth is, I haven't dated enough since the accident to even have a routine."

"And before?" she queried.

"As both of my brothers can attest, there has never been a shortage of women eager to be seen on the arm of a prince. So yes, I dated, and probably more than my fair share. But finding a woman willing to stand by a man who was at sea more than on land was difficult. I can't even remember how many relationships sank when I shipped out, but it was enough that I gave up even trying to make anything work beyond the period of my leave.

"And after I resigned my commission, I didn't meet anyone who made me even think beyond the short-term. Until you."

"We didn't even have short-term," she reminded him. "We had one night."

"We could have more."

Molly shook her head, with sincere regret. "But I appreciate the tour," she said.

She wasn't sure if she was relieved or disappointed that he let the matter drop, as he seemed to do, because he only said, "Then you're pleased with what you've seen of the country so far?"

"I think it would be more appropriate to say I'm both amazed and dazzled."

He smiled. "As I said before, you are welcome to stay on after the wedding to enjoy a real vacation."

She shook her head regretfully. "As tempting as that sounds, I'm afraid nothing here seems real. It's like a postcard-perfect world and a zillion miles away from the realities of my life."

"Has your absence from the restaurant been a problem?" he asked.

"Not at all."

"And it annoys you, at least a little, that all the gears are continuing to turn with the most important cog removed from the machine."

She laughed at his analogy—and because it was true. "It's silly, I know, but you're right."

"It's not silly at all," he denied. "We all like to feel as if we have a purpose in life, a reason for being, and it can be difficult to accept that we aren't as essential as we believed."

She knew he was referring to his own life now, to the career that had abruptly been ended by his injury.

"Do you ever accept it?" she asked, aware that she was prying but unable to stop herself. "Can you ever find another purpose?"

There was more than a touch of wryness in his smile this time. "I'll have to get back to you on that one."

They continued to talk while they ate. The meal began with some kind of chilled soup that was a little bit spicy, followed by a main course of grilled sea bass—apparently one of Genevieve's personal specialties—served with garlic lemon green beans and wild rice, and finished with an assortment of pastries, including slices of a baklava unlike anything Molly had ever tasted.

Through it all, Eric made her feel so comfortable and at ease that when he asked if she wanted to take a walk on the beach after dinner, she didn't even consider refusing.

He left a pile of bills on the table that she guessed more than paid for the meal they'd shared. Then, after a quick stop in the kitchen to thank Genevieve for the incredible meal, they walked toward the water. The sun was only starting to set and the sky was a riot of glorious color. Eric took her hand to help her down the narrow steps that were a public access to the beach, and he didn't let go when they reached the bottom. She didn't protest or tug her hand away. It seemed silly to even consider doing so when they'd shared much deeper intimacies.

They hadn't gone far, however, before she realized that Fiona's sandals weren't very practical on sand, so Molly kicked them off and was pleased when Eric discarded his shoes and socks to walk barefoot with her. They strolled along the water's edge, sometimes talking, sometimes not, but he never let go of her hand.

They were almost back at the stairs when he stopped abruptly.

"Look," he whispered close to her ear.

And her breath caught as she watched the sun complete its descent beyond the horizon.

"I have never seen a sunset like that," she breathed the words quietly, almost reverently.

"And I have never seen anything like you framed by the sunset," he said.

Then his mouth covered hers.

Just like the first time he'd kissed her, his lips were warm and firm, confident in their mastery. There was no tentativeness, no hesitant searching for the right angle, no questioning of her response.

And like the first time, there was no hesitation in her response.

It had been weeks—and yet, it somehow felt as if it was only yesterday. The warm strength of his arms around her wasn't just familiar, it was right. And the explosion of sensations made her mind spin, her heart pound and her body yearn.

He found the pins that held her French twist in place and slipped them free so that her hair spilled into his hands. His fingers sifted through the tresses, caught the ends to tip her head back, changing the angle and deepening the kiss.

She sighed; he groaned.

She wanted him—there was no denying that fact. But she couldn't let herself get caught up in the moment, the romance, the fantasy. There was too much at stake now.

Her system jangled with unacknowledged wants, unsatisfied desires, but she forced herself to take a step back.

"I want to go back to the palace now," she said, though she knew the words were a lie.

What she really wanted was for him to kiss her again, until reality faded away and there was nothing but the two of them. She wanted to make love with him again, to experience the fulfillment she'd only ever known in his arms. But she knew that couldn't happen, not while there was such a huge—and growing—secret between them.

Eric clenched his hands into fists to resist the urge to grab hold of Molly and shake some sense into her. What was it about this woman that she was so determined to deny what was between them?

"Don't you think we should talk about this?"

"It was just a kiss, Eric. I hardly think we need to dissect and analyze every insignificant little detail of it."

His nails dug into his palms. "Maybe it's not necessary," he allowed, somehow managing to match her casual tone despite the fury in his blood, "but I'm curious as to which part you think is most insignificant—your tongue in my mouth, your breasts plastered against my chest or your hips rocking against mine."

Her eyes narrowed even as her cheeks flushed with color. "So I responded to you physically. That doesn't mean I want to fall back into bed with you."

"Oh, you want to," he said, confident it was true. "But for some reason, you're afraid to give in to the chemistry between us."

"I just don't want to make a big deal out of something that isn't," she insisted. "And right now, I really want to go back to the palace so I can go to bed *alone*."

There was more going on, something beneath the surface but he was damned if he could figure it out.

He pulled on his socks and shoved his feet into his shoes, not caring that both were full of sand. The only thing that mattered now was getting Molly back to the palace so he could get away from the woman who was slowly driving him insane.

"Let's go," he said.

She followed silently.

Not a word was spoken as they walked back to the car. As he pulled out of the parking lot, Eric thought that if he lived to be a hundred, he would never understand women.

He knew that was a standard complaint of men around the world, but never had he understood it as he did now. Never had he known a woman like Molly who seemed to delight in sending out mixed signals. One minute she was in his arms, her lips soft and warm beneath his, her body yielding to his, and the next she was pushing him away as if she couldn't stand his touch.

Mi Dios.

His fingers tightened around the steering wheel as he guided the little sports car around the steeply winding curves of Oceanview Drive. Below, the waves crashed against the rocks, but

Eric's own mood was too dark to allow him to pay heed to the vagaries of the sea.

He kept his gaze focused on the road, but he was conscious of Molly seated beside him. He was conscious of the tension in every inch of her body, of the quiet intake of every breath she took, of her subtle and unique scent. And mostly he was conscious of the desire that still thrummed in his blood.

He wanted her—more now even than the first time because he knew how incredible they could be together. And while she'd been kissing him on the beach, he'd been certain she wanted the same thing.

Until she said, "I'm ready to go back to the palace now," in a tone that made it clear she didn't mean to the privacy of his rooms.

And he could respect that. He had no intention of forcing his attentions on a woman who made it clear that she wasn't interested. Except that Molly hadn't made *anything* clear—she'd only made his head spin in circles and his body ache with wanting.

Still, he wasn't going to waste any more time chasing after this woman. She knew what he wanted and he would just have to trust that she would let him know if she ever decided she wanted the same thing.

The touch of her hand on his arm made him jolt.

The fierce grip of cool, clammy fingers eradicated any illusions that she was giving him a signal to do anything but pull over to the side of the road. *Now.*

His gaze swung over, noting the pallor of her skin, the panic in her eyes.

He whipped the car onto the soft shoulder, the tires spitting up gravel.

She flung open the door before he'd completely stopped and raced over to the guardrail. Eric was right behind her, wrapping an arm around her waist and lifting her up so that she could heave over the barrier. And she did—tossing her grilled sea bass back into the ocean.

"Okay?" he asked, when the spasms in her stomach had finally stopped.

She nodded.

Now that the crisis had passed, he was suddenly aware of his arm banded around her ribs, just below the soft curves of her breasts. Of her cute little derriere pressed against his groin. Of her hair, swirling in the wind, tickling his throat, teasing him with the scent of her shampoo. And the sudden stillness of her body that alerted him to the fact that she was just as acutely aware of the intimacy of their positions.

He lowered her feet back to the ground and loosened his hold.

Her fingers curled around the top of the guardrail, gripping the metal barrier as she continued to look out at the sea, looking—he suspected—anywhere but at him.

He returned to the car to retrieve a bottle of water from the first aid kit he habitually carried. "It's not cold but it's wet," he said, twisting off the cap and offering it to her.

She accepted it with a quietly murmured thanks and tipped it to her lips to rinse her mouth, then swallowed a few tentative sips.

"I'm sorry," she said, still not meeting his gaze.

"There's no need to apologize," he told her. "Though you might have warned me you have a tendency toward motion sickness."

"I don't usually," she said, sounding more than a little defensive.

He frowned. "Are you blaming my driving?"

"No," she said. "Maybe it was the fish."

Except that Eric had eaten the same thing she had for dinner, and he knew there was nothing wrong with the way it had been prepared.

"I don't mean that it wasn't cooked properly," she said, knowing Genevieve wouldn't have let the plates out of her kitchen otherwise. "But maybe there was some kind of spice or seasoning that doesn't sit well with me.

"Or maybe I just had too much sun today," she suggested as an alternative. "I spent a few hours by the pool with Fiona earlier."

Which he already knew, of course. He had a clear view of the pool from his windows, and he'd found his gaze straying outside all too frequently because she was there. He also knew she'd spent more time in the shade than the sun and that she'd been wearing a hat.

Yeah, she had all kinds of excuses, as if she was desperate for him to pick one—any one—to believe. And Eric had a sudden, sinking feeling that he knew the real reason for her bout of illness.

And though the possibility made *him* feel a little queasy, it wasn't anything he was prepared to ignore.

"Or maybe you're pregnant."

Chapter Eight

Molly wanted to laugh.

Her sister was always complaining about the cluelessness of men in general and of her husband in particular. No one could accuse Eric Santiago of being clueless—she'd gotten sick once, and he assumed he had all the answers.

Unfortunately for Molly, they were the right answers.

"You're not denying it," he said.

She'd considered doing just that, if only to erase the smug certainty from his tone. But the truth would be only too obvious in a few more months and, ultimately, he had a right to know. She might be annoyed that the decision of when and where to tell him had been taken out of her hands, but she was also relieved that he finally knew.

"No," she finally said. "But it's way too early to be making any big announcement about it, so I'd appreciate it if we could keep this between us."

"It's not that early," he said, obviously having already done some quick mental calculations.

She shook her head. "You're making a lot of assumptions."

"You expect me to believe that the baby's not mine?"

No, but she hadn't expected *him* to assume that it was. She'd still been trying to figure out the best way to tell him about the baby, and to prepare herself for the likelihood that he might deny paternity in the absence of proof. It was what almost any man would do when confronted with the news of an unplanned pregnancy, especially by a woman with whom he'd spent only one night. But she was starting to realize that Eric Santiago rarely did what she expected him to do.

"I'm not ready to have this conversation right now," she said.

"Then when?" he demanded.

"Look, Eric, I know this has caught you off guard, but I want to assure you that I made the decision to have this baby and I will assume full responsibility for him or her."

"¡Cómo infierno!"

She blinked, startled by his vehement outburst—and the fleeting hurt in his eyes.

"We made that baby together, we will be responsible for that baby together."

"You've got to be joking."

"I assure you that I am not."

The calm, unyielding tone worried her. Whatever she'd anticipated when she finally got around to telling him about their baby, it wasn't this.

"Did you really think I was the type of man who would abandon my responsibilities?" he challenged her.

"I didn't think *anything,*" she denied. "But we spent one night together, and at the time, I didn't know what type of man you were at all."

"You should know me a lot better now."

"Not well enough to anticipate how you might respond to the news of an unexpected pregnancy."

"Then I'll tell you—I have no intention of denying paternity. My child will be acknowledged and accepted as mine and he will take his rightful place in line to the throne."

She'd been stunned to learn that the father of her child was a prince, apparently so stunned that she'd somehow failed to reach the logical conclusion that his status meant that his child would be royalty, as well.

But she wasn't so stunned now that she failed to notice that he'd used both the terms *"he"* and *"his."* She'd found herself thinking of the baby in male gender terms, too, but only because she couldn't think of her child as "it." She wondered if it was the same for Eric or if he was hoping the baby was a boy because a male child was more important in the royal family hierarchy.

"And what if it's a girl?" she asked.

He frowned. "It makes no difference to me whether the child is a boy or a girl."

"Would it make any difference with respect to succession?"

"No. When Alexandria was born, Julian persuaded parliament to change the law to allow for equal primogeniture so that she wouldn't lose her place in line to the throne, which she would have done when Damon was born.

"Which means," he continued, "regardless of the child's gender, he or she will come directly after me in the line of succession."

"And where are you in the line?" she asked, starting to feel a little weak in the knees at the thought that her unborn child could someday rule a Mediterranean country.

"Seventh," he answered her question.

The response helped her to breathe again because she knew,

realistically, that while her child's place in line to the throne meant he *could* someday rule the country, it was unlikely he would ever be called upon do so.

Still—a mother who was a bartender and a father who was a prince? If that wasn't a recipe for disaster for the poor kid, she didn't know what was.

Molly was quiet during the rest of the drive back to the palace. Too quiet, Eric thought, as he maneuvered the vehicle slowly along the winding coastal road, casting frequent glances in her direction to make sure she was okay.

He felt guilty for coming on so strong, but it had seriously irritated him that she could believe—for even half a second—he might not want his child.

As for the paternity issue, he knew there would be some who'd expect him to demand proof before accepting that the child Molly carried was his. He didn't need proof because he knew Molly—obviously a lot better than she knew him.

She hadn't been a virgin when they'd made love, but it had been readily apparent to Eric that her experience was limited. She'd responded to every brush of his lips and touch of his hands with soft sighs and quiet gasps that were filled with wonder. She had been both shy and eager, hesitant and willing, and the contradiction between her obvious desire and innocence had been incredibly arousing.

Glancing at her now, he saw that her hands were folded in her lap, her gaze locked upon them, and he remembered what Fiona had told him about Molly's reluctance to let anyone get close. He was going to have to tread more carefully than he'd done so far if she was going to open up to him.

"I know you aren't ready to make any big decisions right now," he said. "But we are going to have to talk about this sometime."

She nibbled on her bottom lip. "Can it wait until after the wedding?"

He frowned, thinking of her intention to return to Texas right after Scott and Fiona were married, and conscious of the clock that was ticking.

"Will you agree to stay for a while after the wedding?" he asked again.

"For what purpose?"

"To give us a chance to figure this out and make plans for our own."

She turned her head to look at him. "Our own what?"

"Wedding."

"What? No. No way."

"You might want to give the idea some thought before you discard it out of hand."

"*You* need to give it some thought," she told him. "Because if you did, you'd realize the idea is crazy."

As far as proposals went, he realized this one left a lot to be desired. But he felt it was important to communicate what he wanted, and in that first moment when he'd realized Molly was carrying his child, he'd known.

He wanted Molly and the baby.

Their baby.

The rush of fierce possessiveness that swept through him drowned everything else.

"I want to be a father to this child," he said, in case he hadn't already made that point perfectly clear. "And the best way to ensure that is for us to get married."

"Marriage doesn't ensure anything."

"I'm not asking for an answer right now. I'm just asking you to think about it."

"The answer is no. I don't want my child growing up in a fishbowl, and your need to don a disguise when we went into town this afternoon made me realize that the child of a prince—"

"Whether or not we marry," he interrupted, "our child will be a member of the royal family."

"We are not going to marry," she said firmly.

Eric knew that if he pushed her any further right now, she'd only dig in her heels, so he let the subject drop, confident that she would eventually come around to his way of thinking.

When they'd left the palace a few hours earlier, he'd been looking forward to a pleasant afternoon and some time alone with Molly. He hadn't been expected to be hit with the knowledge that he was going to be a father—or to already be thinking of marriage to the mother of his child. And while this situation was definitely outside the realm of his experience, he didn't feel overwhelmed or trapped or panicked. Maybe it was because so much of his life had been turned upside down in the past few years that he was able to take these new developments in stride, but whatever the reason, marrying Molly just seemed...right.

Marcus would probably say he was still suffering the lingering effects of the concussion he'd sustained three years earlier. Of course, Marcus had always been quick with the jokes, and quicker to extricate himself from any relationship with a woman who had even hinted at long-term—at least until he met Jewel.

Unlike his younger brother, Eric had never been opposed to the idea of marriage. He'd just never had reason to consider it. But he was going to do more than consider it now.

There was going to be another royal wedding in Tesoro del Mar—just as soon as he could convince the woman he wished to become his bride.

Molly was relieved when she woke up the next morning and found a note from her cousin telling her that Fiona and Scott had borrowed a car and were taking a drive to the other side of the island. She was grateful for the reprieve, temporary though she knew it would be. Having succeeded in sending Molly and Eric off together the day before, Fiona would want to hear all the details of their outing, and Molly wasn't quite sure how she would answer her questions.

She imagined Eric would give her a wide berth today. Not just because of the friction between them but because he would need some time to figure out what he really wanted with respect to a relationship with his child.

In the light of day, Molly realized she shouldn't have been so surprised by his impulsive proposal the night before. She knew he was an honorable man who took his responsibilities seriously. It would be natural for him to want to assume responsibility for his child. But she was equally convinced that, having had an opportunity to think it through, he would be grateful she hadn't accepted his offer of marriage.

She went down to the dining room for breakfast, helping herself to a bowl of fresh fruit and a muffin. It seemed that everyone else had already been and gone and though she didn't mind the solitude, she was conscious of the fact that she'd slept late every morning since arriving on the island and worried that she would become accustomed to this life of leisure. Long stretches of time in which she was required to do absolutely nothing were beyond her realm of experience, so she was pleased when she wandered into the garden and found Princess Lara there with her sons.

Matthew had a butterfly net in one hand and a bug box in the other and was bent at the waist, peering intently at the grass. William toddled around behind his brother, his steps a little unsteady on the grass. Occasionally he'd land on his diaper-clad bottom, but he'd just push himself up again and keep going, though he frequently looked back to make sure his mother was still there and never ventured too far away from her.

"We're looking for frogs," the three-year-old young prince informed Molly when she joined them. "Would you like to help?"

"Frogs?" Molly squatted down so that she was at eye level with him. "What kind—brown ones or green ones?"

His little brow furrowed and he looked to his mother for help.

"Whichever ones we can find," she told him, before lowering her voice so that only Molly could hear and adding, "which I'm hoping is none."

Molly smiled at the princess, then turned back to the little boy and asked, "Are there any purple ones around here?"

"There's no such thing as purple frogs," he said authoritatively.

"How do you know?"

"'Cause Damon's caught lotsa frogs and he's never caught a purple one."

"And I've told you," Lara reminded her son, "just because you haven't seen something doesn't mean it doesn't exist."

"So there are purple frogs?"

Lara shrugged. "I've never seen one, but who knows?"

He turned to Molly. "Are there purple ones?"

"I can't say for sure, either," she admitted. "But I've heard about them and that they're magical frogs."

His eyes lit up. "Magical?"

Molly nodded. "If you're lucky enough to find one, you pick it up—very gently, of course—and hold it in the palm of your hand for the count of ten. Can you count to ten?"

His head bobbed up and down enthusiastically.

"Okay, so you count slowly and out loud and when you get to ten, it will roll over onto its back so you can see its belly—which is actually more pink than purple—and make a wish as you tickle his belly."

"What kind of wish?"

"Any kind of wish you want."

"And my wish will come true?"

"That's what they say. But," she cautioned, "it only works if you haven't touched any other frogs that day—not green ones or brown ones and especially not blue ones."

His eyes grew wide. "There's blue ones, too?"

Molly nodded.

"Wow." He turned to his mom. "I'm goin' huntin' for purple frogs," he said, and raced off again, lugging both the butterfly net and the bug box.

"Why especially not the blue ones?" Lara wondered, her voice tinged with both admiration and amusement.

"Because the blue ones are poison to the purple ones and when the purple ones get sick, they can't grant anyone's wishes."

Lara laughed and dropped down onto the grass beside Molly. "You certainly piqued my son's interest."

Molly shrugged. "Kids are always a great audience."

"I'd say you're a great storyteller. Ever put any of your ideas on paper?"

She shook her head.

"Why not?" the princess asked.

"Because I'm a bartender, not a writer."

"You have a gift," Lara insisted. "It would be a shame not to see what you could do with it."

Molly's grandmother had said the same thing to her more than once, but she'd thought she was just encouraging her because that's what grandmothers did—and because hers in particular thought she should be doing anything other than serving drinks in a bar. But Molly had never really thought seriously of doing anything else, so she was relieved when William crawled over and drew Lara's attention.

The baby climbed into his mother's lap and laid his head against her breast, rubbing his eyes with hands that were stained with dirt and grass. Lara just sighed and snuggled him closer. "You're getting sleepy, aren't you, dirty boy?"

His only response was a yawn.

Molly felt a strange tug inside her as she realized it wouldn't be too much longer before she would have her own baby to cuddle in her arms.

"They're all such stunning children," she murmured.

"The Santiago genes are strong," Lara said, then smiled. "And exceptional."

Molly nodded. "I met Prince Damon first," she said. "And I was stunned by how beautiful he is. I know he's a boy, but there isn't any other word to do him justice. I thought the same thing when I saw his brother and then Prince Matthew and Prince William, too. And then Princess Alexandria walked into the room and somehow managed to outshine them all."

Lara laughed. "She does, doesn't she? And Isabella, Marcus and Jewel's baby, is just the same. You'll get to meet her when they fly in for the wedding."

"They're coming here for Scott and Fiona's wedding?"

"Yeah, Marcus grumbled, of course, because San Antonio is a lot closer to West Virginia than Tesoro del Mar is, but I don't think he would miss it for the world."

"I didn't realize, until recently, that Scott had grown up here," Molly said. "I'm not sure Fiona did, either, or knew that his best friend was a prince. I mean, Scott had talked about Eric and Marcus and Rowan, but he certainly didn't make a big deal out of the fact that they were royalty."

"Titles shouldn't matter between friends," the princess said simply. "Which is why I'd really like it if you'd call me 'Lara' instead of 'Your Highness'."

"Thank you," Molly said.

Lara rose to her feet with the half asleep baby on her shoulder and grinned. "And as your friend," she said. "I expect to be kept apprised of whatever is going on between you and Eric—because I know there's something."

Molly couldn't deny it, but she could clarify to ensure the princess didn't anticipate any new romantic developments. "Was."

The smile never wavered. "We'll see about that."

And before Molly could think of an appropriate response, Lara had excused herself to round up Matthew, and take both kids inside, to clean them up before they went for their naps.

Despite the hints about Molly's relationship with Eric, she'd enjoyed the time she'd spent with the princess and her children and was disappointed when they left.

Left to her own devices once again, she changed into her bathing suit, slathered on a generous amount of sunscreen and headed down to the pool. She'd forgotten to pack a book and considered detouring past the library on the main level to borrow one, but decided that she wasn't feeling that ambitious. She didn't want to read or think…she just wanted to be.

She laid her towel over the back of the lounge chair, adjusted the tilt and settled in. Then she remembered Fiona's warning about raccoon eyes and tan lines, so she removed her sunglasses and, double-checking to make sure no one else was around, she untied the strings of the halter from around her neck and tucked them into the keyhole between her breasts.

She promised herself that she would clear her mind, that she wouldn't let herself think about Eric or her pregnancy or anything else that would give her worry lines. And she managed to keep that promise—until a shadow fell over her, blocking the sun.

She knew, even before she opened her eyes, that it was Eric. Somehow, instinctively, she just knew.

"How long have you been out here?" he asked her.

She shrugged, then realized her mistake when the top of her bathing suit slipped a little lower.

His gaze dropped, lingered.

"The dress I'm wearing for the wedding is strapless," she explained. "Fiona would have a fit if I had tan lines."

"I imagine she would." He reached for the bottle of sunscreen beside her chair, squirted some on his palm, then rubbed his hands together to spread it over both. "She would be even more upset if you burned."

Molly swallowed as he shifted closer, his intent obvious. "I covered up pretty good before I came out."

"But you don't even know how long you've been out," he said, sliding his hands over the curve of her shoulders.

She had to bite down on her lip so that she wouldn't moan out loud because, oh my, he had such talented hands. Such wickedly, wonderfully, talented hands.

No—she wouldn't moan. But she would, and did, close her eyes, as he smoothed lotion down her arms, then up again. Across her collarbone. And—oh my—over the swell of her breasts.

Desire, hot and liquid, pulsed through her system as his hands glided over her skin, caressing and lingering long after the lotion had been rubbed into her skin.

"I think that's, um, good," she finally managed. "Thanks."

His lips curved. "My pleasure."

"So..." she held a hand over her eyes, shielding them from the sun as she looked up at him "...is there a reason you came down to the pool? Because it obviously wasn't to swim."

"I sat in on a meeting with the Minister of Economic Development," he said, explaining the dark suit he wore. "I came down to the pool looking for you."

"And now you've found me."

"So I did," he agreed, then grinned. "The question now is, can I keep you?"

"Believe me, you won't want to in a few more months."

"I can't imagine that being true," he said, sitting on the edge of the chair beside hers. "Just thinking about the fact that you're carrying my baby—"

"Eric," she warned.

"There's no one around to overhear."

He was right. They were completely alone. It was just the two of them and all of her rampaging hormones—*not* a good scenario.

"And as I was saying," he continued, "just knowing that you're carrying my child makes me want you even more."

"The wanting is what got us into this predicament," she reminded him.

"Yeah," he agreed, and gave her another one of those slow smiles that made everything inside of her turn to mush.

Molly picked up her glass and drank deeply, but what had been ice water half an hour before was now lukewarm and did nothing to cool the heat in her veins.

As the day of Fiona and Scott's wedding drew nearer, Molly saw less and less of Eric. She knew that all the details for the wedding had been taken care of so there was no reason for him to hang around. No reason except that he'd said they would figure things out together and it was kind of hard to figure things out with somebody who was never around.

She knew he was involved in meetings with the Minister of Economic Development and that those meetings were somehow related to the potential expansion of Scott's business, but to Molly, it was just further proof that she couldn't rely on anyone but herself. And even she wasn't so dependable these days, with the way her mind was spinning in circles contemplating all of the possibilities—go back to Texas/stay in Tesoro del Mar/return to her job/sell the restaurant/buy a time-share in Timbuktu.

Okay, so maybe that last option wasn't a realistic one, but she was so desperate for a solution, she was willing to consider almost anything.

Anything except marriage.

Not that Eric had brought up the subject since the night he'd first learned that she was pregnant, which led her to hope that he'd come to his senses. And she was grateful for that. The last thing she needed or wanted was to be pressured into marriage by a man who was intent on doing "the right thing."

But what did she want?

Unfortunately, that was a question to which she didn't have an answer.

Chapter Nine

Eric sat at a table in the corner, a beer in hand, and watched Molly on the dance floor.

He'd been watching her all night, unable to take his eyes off of her since she'd walked down the aisle ahead of Fiona at the start of the ceremony earlier in the evening. He'd always known she was beautiful, but tonight she was simply stunning.

He'd been forewarned by their conversation by the pool a few days earlier that the dress was strapless, but that had hardly been sufficient information to prepare him for the image she presented in the slim column of sapphire silk that shimmered like blue flame when she moved.

The vibrant color made her skin look even creamier, her eyes even bluer. Her dark hair was swept up off her neck and piled on top of her head in some kind of fancy style that tempted him to pluck the pins free so the silky tresses would spill into his hands.

Yeah, he'd been watching her all night and enjoying every minute—until he saw Cameron Leandres approach. His cousin said a few words, Molly smiled, and the next thing Eric knew, they were on the dance floor together.

"You're going to break that glass if you're not careful," Marcus warned from behind him.

Eric forced his fingers to relax and pushed the drink away as his brother pulled out a chair and joined him.

"What is he even doing here?" Eric demanded.

"Cameron?"

"Yeah, Cameron."

"Scott invited him," Marcus said. "Michael and Samantha are here, too."

Eric knew that and he didn't have any issue with his other cousin and his cousin's wife being there, but Michael's younger brother was a different story.

"And you're okay with this?" he asked Marcus now.

His brother shrugged. "It's not my wedding, is it?"

"But this is our home."

"And Cameron is, as much as we'd sometimes like to pretend otherwise, part of our family."

"Yeah—the part that tried to create a scandal and undermine Rowan's authority as prince regent, and then drive a wedge between you and Jewel by revealing that you'd been working at her training center under an assumed identity."

"*Tried* being the operative word," Marcus reminded him.

"And now he's trying to put the moves on Molly," Eric grumbled.

"Are you worried that she's the type to succumb to his questionable charms?"

"No," he said, and he wasn't. "I just don't want him getting any ideas about my future wife."

Marcus choked on his beer.

Eric thumped him on the back, probably a little harder than was necessary.

"Geez," Marcus grumbled. "You should give a guy some warning before you drop a bomb like that."

"Is it really such a shock?"

"The idea of you wanting to marry a woman you've only known a few weeks?"

Eric picked up his beer again, took a long swallow. "Actually, I've known her a little bit longer than that."

His brother's eyes narrowed. "How much longer?"

"A few months."

"The first time you were out in Texas," Marcus guessed. "Lara said you'd met someone there."

"When did she tell you that?"

"When she called and suggested I drop by to visit you in San Antonio and try to wrangle an introduction."

"Because San Antonio is just around the corner from Alliston," Eric noted dryly.

"But she was right, wasn't she?"

"She was right," he admitted.

"So you've known Molly a few months," Marcus picked up the earlier thread of their conversation. "That's still no reason to rush into talking about marriage, unless..." his voice trailed off as realization dawned "...she's pregnant."

Eric knew Molly wasn't ready to make any announcements about the baby they were expecting, but this was his brother and Eric wasn't going to lie to him.

"Due January seventh," he admitted. "And while I expect to have my ring on her finger long before then, I'd appreciate it if you didn't say anything about the baby to anyone else."

Marcus nodded and lifted his bottle again. As he took another swallow of his beer, Eric knew what he was thinking, and the he was debating the wisdom of speaking those thoughts aloud.

"Yes," he said, before Marcus could piss him off by asking the question. "I'm sure it's mine."

"Well, then—" his brother lifted his glass "—congratulations."

Eric nodded. "Thanks." He finished his drink. "Just one thing?"

"What's that?"

"Don't say anything about my plans to the bride-to-be."

"She doesn't know there's going to be a wedding?" Marcus guessed.

"Not yet."

Marcus lifted his glass again. "Good luck with that."

Eric suspected he was going to need it.

By the time midnight rolled around and the bride and groom were whisked away to the airport, Molly was exhausted. But as she waved to the departing couple in the limousine, she was happy for her cousin, and more uncertain than ever about her own future.

She felt Eric's presence before she turned her head and saw him standing behind her.

The intensity in his gaze made her heart pound a little faster, but she managed a smile and said, "You did it."

His brows lifted. "What did I do?"

"You made sure this was a day that Scott and Fiona will never forget."

"I wish I could take the credit," he said. "But really, I only delegated jobs to those who were much more capable of doing them."

"Then you delegated well."

"Thank you." He offered her his arm, and she took it, and they wandered to the back gardens together.

"Did you want to walk?" he asked her.

"Actually, I would love to just sit for a few minutes," she told him. "I feel as if I've been on my feet all day."

"Then we'll sit," he said, and led her over to the stone bench by the fountain.

The ballroom doors had been thrown open and she could hear the band still playing for the few guests that remained. She imagined the revelry might go on for quite a while yet, but she was more than ready to hang up her dancing shoes for the night.

"I told Marcus about the baby."

"Oh."

The disappointment in her tone was obvious. "You don't sound pleased."

She shrugged. "I thought we agreed we wouldn't tell anyone yet."

"He's not anyone, he's my brother," Eric explained. "And in all fairness, he sort of guessed. Have you really told no one?"

"Only you."

"Not even your sister?"

"*Especially* not my sister."

Eric was surprised by this response. While he understood that she wasn't ready to make a public announcement about her pregnancy, he thought she'd be anxious to share the news with her family.

"Abbey had a miscarriage five months ago," she told him. "Actually, it was her third miscarriage in eight years of trying to have a baby."

He could only imagine how painful each experience must have been for her sister, and he was concerned that there was something in the family history that might affect Molly's pregnancy, as well.

"Do they know why she miscarried?" he asked cautiously.

"They have some theories, none of which are genetic, and my

GP assured me that there's no reason to worry that I can't carry this baby to term."

"You haven't seen a specialist?"

"I had an appointment to see an ob-gyn, but I had to cancel it when Scott and Fiona's wedding plans got changed. I'll reschedule when I get back."

"You could see someone here," he suggested. "I could get the name of Lara's doctor… No, I guess I can't without explaining why I'd need it." And if Eric took Molly to an ob-gyn in Tesoro del Mar, the news of her pregnancy would undoubtedly be headlines the very next morning.

"I'll be home within a week, anyway," she reminded him.

Which was another subject he wanted to discuss with her, but he opted to wait. They were actually having a civil conversation and he didn't want to ruin it by asking for something he knew she wasn't ready to consider.

"How have you been feeling?" he asked.

"I'm fine," she assured him. "I promise."

"No morning sickness?"

"Only that one very memorable incident."

He smiled, but his gaze was serious when he asked, "And if I hadn't figured it out—were you going to tell me?"

She nodded. "I was just trying to work out the how and when."

He reached for her hand, linked their fingers together. "From now on, we'll figure our future out together, okay?"

"I think it's important that we work together for the sake of our child, but I don't see that we have a future beyond that."

"Only because you're not looking," he chided. "I want to marry you, Molly."

"Haven't we been through this already?"

"I know it came as a surprise when I mentioned it the first time, but now that you've had some time to think about it, I'd hoped you would have considered the benefits."

"And I hoped, after you'd had some time to think about it, you'd realize how ridiculous the idea is."

"What's so ridiculous about it?" he demanded.

"For starters, how about the fact that we don't even know one another?"

"We know one another a lot better now than we did a few months ago."

"Not nearly well enough to promise till death do us part'."

"We're going to have a baby together," he reminded her. "We'll have plenty of time to get to know one another."

It occurred to her then that he honestly didn't understand why she wasn't thrilled with his "proposal." She didn't know if it was because he was a prince that he expected to get what he wanted when he wanted it, but she knew they would continue to have the same argument about marriage if she didn't make him understand her feelings on the subject.

"Do you know what made today so perfect for Scott and Fiona?" she finally asked.

He looked at her warily. "I thought it was my exceptional delegating skills."

She managed a smile. "No, your exceptional delegating skills ensured that it will be remembered fondly by all of the guests as a beautiful wedding. But what made it perfect for the bride and groom was the way they looked at each other when they spoke their vows, as if there was no one else around, as if nothing else could ever matter as much as their love for and commitment to one another."

She took his hands, willing him to understand. "If I ever get married, it will be because I feel the same way about someone, not because it's the logical or reasonable thing to do."

"Do you really think love guarantees a successful marriage?"

"No," she admitted. "But at least it gives a solid foundation to build on."

"What about attraction?" he challenged.

"What about it?"

"Do you agree that sexual attraction is important in a relationship?"

"Of course, but—"

He touched his fingers to her mouth, halting her words and making her lips tingle and her heart pound.

"'Of course' is all the answer I need for now." His fingertips traced the curve of her lips, first the top, then the bottom, then across the seam.

She shivered, sighed.

He smiled.

"And we have sexual attraction, don't we?"

She could hardly deny it, not when her blood was pulsing like molten lava through her veins and her knees were actually trembling in response to his nearness.

His fingers dropped away from her lips, skimmed over her chin, down her throat and lower, to the hollow between her breasts.

"Don't we?" he asked again.

She could only nod as his fingers caressed the bare skin above the neckline of her dress, creating little sparks of pleasure everywhere he touched.

"The last time I kissed you, you pushed me away."

She swallowed. "I kissed you back first."

He smiled. "Yeah, you did."

His fingers continued their gentle, torturous stroking.

"If I kiss you now…will you push me away…or kiss me back?"

She lifted her arms to his shoulders, her hands diving into the soft thickness of his hair to pull his head down to her.

"Let's find out."

She whispered the words against his mouth, then sank her teeth into his bottom lip and tugged gently.

The unexpected action surprised him—and aroused him unbearably.

His arms banded around her waist, and he yanked her tight against his body so that her breasts were crushed against his chest, her thighs trapped between his. She moaned, but he knew it wasn't a sound of protest but of yearning, that the heat that had been simmering between them for so long was about to burst into flame.

She tore her lips from his only long enough to say, "Let's go inside."

It was what he wanted more than anything, and he glanced up at the sky to say, "*Gracias, Dios.*"

Then he took her hand and they raced down the path, staying in the shadows so no one would see them sneaking in through the garden entrance together.

His rooms had never seemed so far away as they did tonight, and when they finally reached the fourth floor, they were both breathless. He flipped the lock on the door and tugged her into his arms.

His hands slid up her back, finding the pull of the zipper between her shoulder blades, sliding it down. The fabric parted and his fingers dipped inside to caress the skin beneath, skim lightly over the delicate bumps of her spine. The sensual caress made her shiver, an involuntary response that caused the tips of her breasts to rub against his chest so that he felt the nipples pebble even through the taffeta silk.

Unable to resist any longer, he pushed the bodice of her dress down, baring her breasts. He dipped his head to kiss and suckle, enjoying the increased fullness and sensitivity, making her squirm with every tweak and lick and nibble.

He pushed the garment lower, over the flare of her hips, so that it pooled at her feet, leaving her clad in only a tiny pair of panties and pencil-thin heels.

"He muerto y he ido al cielo."

He didn't realize he'd spoken out loud until her lips curved, just a little.

A siren's body and an innocent's smile—he had never known a woman with so many inherent contradictions. He had never wanted a woman as he wanted Molly.

She started unbuttoning his shirt; he yanked it out of his pants and tossed it aside as they moved toward the bedroom, shedding the rest of his clothes along the way.

He tumbled her onto the bed; she pulled him down with her, wrapping her legs around him, anchoring their bodies together.

With a quick tug, he tore away the lace panties. She gasped with shock, then moaned when he cupped her. She was wet and willing and he was desperate to have her.

He automatically reached toward the night table for a condom, the habit so deeply ingrained it didn't occur to him not to until Molly took the packet from his hand and tossed it aside as carelessly as he had her panties.

He got the message—the fact that she was already pregnant nullified at least one of the purposes of protection. And he'd seen so many doctors and had so many tests over the past few years he knew there were no concerns about his health, and he trusted that Molly wouldn't have dispensed with the little square package if there were any issues on her side.

Still, her action gave him pause, making him realize that he had never made love to a woman without a layer of latex separating them. But it was how he wanted Molly—with no barriers of any kind between them.

He grasped her hips and drove into her slick heat. She arched and accepted. They moved together in a perfectly choreographed rhythm until her muscles clamped around him, gripping him like a velvet glove, holding him tight, dragging him over the precipice with her.

* * *

They barely let go of one another through the night. He brought her to climax more times than she could remember, so that even while her body still trembled with the after-effects, she'd quivered with anticipation.

She knew it wasn't just the sexual release that she'd needed. It was Eric in her arms, inside of her, filling and fulfilling her. When he was with her, she felt the link, not just physical but emotional, he filled her body and her heart and her soul.

She arched against him, mindlessly, desperately seeking the completion she knew he could give her. She had never given up control easily, but she gave it up to him now, relinquished it happily.

With every sweep of his hands, every touch of his lips, every brush of his body against hers, he made her sigh and gasp and moan. She thought she should know what to expect by now, but though their bodies came together with an ease and familiarity that spoke of passions already shared, each time was different, each experience added new layers of sensation that were somehow deeper, sharper, sweeter than before.

It was exciting, exhilarating—and terrifying.

In his bed, in his arms, she felt safe, secure, protected. In his arms, she could almost believe that a relationship between them might work.

And what scared her the most was that she didn't want to leave—and that was why she had to go.

Chapter Ten

Eric wasn't surprised when he woke up alone.

He didn't think Molly was ready for anyone to know that they were together, and though he hoped to change her mind about that in the very near future, he was feeling too happy this morning to worry about it right now.

Rowan and Lara were already in the dining room when he went down for breakfast. Lara was feeding oatmeal to William who seemed to enjoy spitting it back at her, inciting Matthew to spit his cereal back into his bowl—until his father caught him in the act, which made Eric smile. It was always chaos when the whole family was together—and he absolutely loved it.

Marcus and Jewel wandered in a few minutes later, his younger brother with his baby daughter tucked in the crook of one arm and his other around his wife. And it occurred to Eric that in a little more than seven months, there would be yet another baby at the table—and hopefully another royal bride before then.

When Maria came in to see what he wanted for breakfast, he said, "Just coffee right now, thanks. I'll eat with Ms. Shea when she comes down."

"Of course, Your Highness." She filled his cup. "I'll wait until she returns."

Eric froze with his cup halfway to his mouth. "Returns?"

But Maria had already gone back into the kitchen.

Eric looked around the table, noting that all other conversations seemed to have stopped so that the only sound was William banging his plastic spoon against the edge of his bowl.

It was Lara who finally broke the silence. "She was up early, with her suitcases packed, and asked for the number of a local taxi service. Luis drove her to the airport."

He set his cup carefully back into the saucer. "What time was that?"

"About half an hour—maybe forty-five minutes—ago." Her eyes were filled with sympathy and compassion. "I'm sorry, I assumed you knew of her plans."

"I didn't," he admitted grimly.

"There seems to be a lot of that going around," Marcus noted, amusement in his tone.

"For your information, I did tell her of my plans last night," he told his brother.

"Apparently that went over well."

Marcus's comment was immediately followed by Rowan asking, "Do you want to fill the rest of us in?"

But Eric was already pushing his chair away from the table. "Not right now."

"Well, I wish someone would," Jewel said. "Because I feel like I walked into the middle of a play in the second act."

"You haven't," he heard her husband console. "In fact, I'd bet the action is just about to begin."

* * *

Molly sat on the end of a row of linked chairs facing the ticket counter. On the vacant seat beside her was a discarded newspaper—*La Noticia, Edición Especial*—with the headline A Palace Wedding.

Curious, she picked up the paper and smiled at the photo of Fiona and Scott standing in front of the minister, their hands linked, their happiness radiating even from the page. She skimmed the brief article about the wedding, which outlined Scott's longtime connection with the royal family and briefly summarized his courtship of the former Miss Texas.

Additional coverage was on page two, but when Molly turned the page, she was stunned by the headline there.

WHO IS MOLLY SHEA?
by Alex Girard

Little is known about the slim, raven-haired woman who stood as maid of honor for her cousin, Fiona Gilmore, when she married communications magnate Scott Delsey in a sunset ceremony at the palace yesterday afternoon. But it was obvious that the Texas beauty had captured the attention of not only one but two members of the royal family—His Royal Highness Eric Santiago and his cousin, Prince Cameron Leandres.

The brother of the prince regent couldn't seem to take his eyes off of the woman in sapphire silk, while the son of the princess royal couldn't wait to get his hands on her (see photos below). Will another heir to the throne choose an American bride? Only time—and *La Noticia*—will tell, because the prospect of another royal romance has definitely caught *our* attention.

* * *

The photos were clear—the first of Molly and Eric flanking the bride and groom respectively as they exchanged their vows, the next of Molly and Cameron dancing. She was more amused than annoyed by the coverage, though she could see how such attention could become tiresome if endured on a daily basis, as she knew it was by members of the royal family. And it was just one more reason she needed to leave Tesoro del Mar.

She stuffed the paper in the side pocket of her carry-on so that no one else could pick it up and possibly identify her as the woman in the photos, but still made no move toward the ticket counter.

The screen displaying travel information confirmed a nine-fifteen flight to Miami with a connection through to San Antonio, and if she booked a ticket, she could be on that flight and home in time for dinner. She *wanted* to be home, where she wouldn't be tempted to give in to her dreams about dark-eyed princes. And yet there was a part of her that already regretted slipping out of Eric's bed without giving him any hint of her intentions.

He'd asked her stay—to give them a chance to build a relationship. And it was her desire to do exactly that, that had scared her away.

She knew he'd be angry when he woke up and found she was gone. She also knew that running away was nothing more than a temporary solution. He would come after her—she didn't doubt that for a minute. He wanted to be part of their child's life and he wouldn't let her shut him out. But she didn't want to shut him out—she just wanted to be wanted, too.

No, that wasn't exactly true, either. If it was, she would be content to stay, because Eric had shown he numerous times throughout the night that she was wanted. What she needed was to be loved, as she was starting to love him.

All of her excuses about having to go back because of the restaurant were just that—excuses. She was leaving Tesoro del Mar because she was afraid to go after what she really wanted, because she was afraid that, once again, she might lose everything that mattered.

And, she realized now, all of her reasons for running were about *her*—her wants and needs, her fears and insecurities. It was time to consider the needs of her child ahead of her own, and didn't she owe it to the baby she carried to give him the best possible relationship with *both* parents?

She kept thinking about her responsibilities at the restaurant, but what about her responsibilities to her child? Shouldn't the most important consideration be what was best for her baby?

The ring of her cell jolted her from her thoughts. Her first thought was *Eric,* and her heart pounded with equal parts anticipation and trepidation as she pulled the phone from her purse. But the number on the display belonged to her sister, which gave her pause.

Throughout her internal debate of whether to stay or go, she'd failed to think of how her decision would affect the other people in her life. She wanted to go home and pick her life up where everything was steady and familiar. But having a baby changed everything—there would be no steady and familiar. And she didn't want to flaunt her pregnancy in the face of her sister, who yearned so desperately for a child of her own.

"Are you up really early or really late?" she asked.

"Early," Abbey admitted. "After being woken up by a long-distance telephone call from a reporter."

Molly wiped her clammy hands down the front of her skirt. "A reporter?"

"You didn't know he was going to call?"

"Why would I?"

"Because he was asking about you."

Her heart sank. "What did you tell him?"

"Nothing, really. At least, I don't think so. I was caught completely off guard by the call."

"What did he ask you?"

"First he wanted to know how long you'd been dating Prince Eric, and, well, I was kind of surprised by the question because I didn't even know you were dating him."

"I'm not."

"Oh, okay," Abbey said, sounding relieved that she hadn't been kept in the dark about something so potentially momentous. "Then he asked about your relationship with someone named Prince Cameron, and I had to admit I'd never even heard of him."

Molly exhaled a sigh of relief at this confirmation that her sister hadn't told the reporter anything, but she was still unnerved that he'd even called to ask about her when she'd done nothing to warrant any interest. Okay, she'd slept with a prince—twice now—but no one besides she and Eric knew about those nights they'd spent together.

"Is there something going on that I should know?" Abbey asked now.

"No," Molly said. Then, to distract her sister, she asked, "How are things at home?"

"Good," Abbey answered without hesitation, more eager to talk about her own life than speculate about her sister's. "I mean *really* good, even though I'm not sure how or why things have changed. Jason says that *I* have—that this getting out and meeting people has been good for me. And maybe he's right, because even after I finished my shift last night, I hung around to help out at the bar and we got to talking—I mean, *really* talking, like we haven't talked in a long time. And I really feel as if we're back on track with our marriage."

"That's great, Abbey."

"I know I was upset when you left. I felt as if you were abandoning me when I really needed you, but now I realize you did me a favor. I wouldn't have learned that I could stand on my own two feet if I was always leaning on you."

"But that's what family's for," Molly said.

"Except somewhere along the way I lost sight of the fact that Jason's my family, too, and that we need to be there for one another. Like he tried to be there for me, after the last miscarriage, when I pushed him away. I just felt like such a failure as a woman and a wife."

"You've been through a lot," Molly said sympathetically.

"It was a really rough patch for me," Abbey agreed. "But I'm okay now, and I'm ready to try again."

"Are you sure that's a good idea?"

Her sister huffed out an impatient breath. "Now you sound like my husband. Of course I'm sure. We're never going to have the baby we want if we don't keep trying."

Molly had accompanied her sister to enough specialist appointments to know it wasn't that simple. The doctors had been honest and up-front with Abbey about that—she just refused to accept that she might never have a baby.

So Molly changed the subject by telling her sister about the ceremony on the beach and dancing in the mirrored ballroom, and Abbey sighed, caught up in the romance of it all.

"It sounds like you're having a great time."

"It was incredible," she admitted.

"I wouldn't blame you if you weren't in a hurry to come home," her sister said. "And if you wanted to stay awhile, take a bit of a vacation, Jason and I can handle everything at Shea's."

Molly smiled at the not-so-subtle hint.

And though there was a part of her that actually ached to be home, to fall back into the comfort and routine of her life before Eric, she accepted that nothing would ever again be the same as it was before, and that going back to Texas might not be the best thing for her or her sister right now.

Because if she went home, she'd have to tell Abbey about her pregnancy, and she wasn't ready to say the words she knew would break her sister's heart. Not when Abbey was doing so well getting her life back on track.

But if she stayed, and any reporters saw her spending time with Eric, it wouldn't take them long to figure out she was carrying Eric's baby when her pregnancy became apparent. And then she would be like a goldfish trapped in a bowl. On the other hand, if she went back to Texas now and Eric followed her, nothing would change except the venue, and she didn't want to play out any kind of drama in front of her family. Despite everything that Abbey had done to hurt her in the past, she wasn't looking for payback and she didn't want the news that she was carrying a royal baby splashed across the headlines.

It was that possibility that convinced her to stay in Tesoro del Mar. At least for a while.

"It's funny you should mention a vacation," she said.

"Because?" Abbey prompted.

"Because..." Her response trailed off as she registered the sound of brisk footsteps with a sudden flurry of excited whispers from the travelers around her. Glancing up, she saw Eric, flanked by the two bodyguards that habitually accompanied him into public venues. She forced herself to focus, even as the butterflies in her tummy were kicking up a serious ruckus. "Because I was planning to call and tell you that I've decided to stay in Tesoro del Mar for a while longer."

She didn't hear Abbey's response. She didn't hear anything over the pounding of her own heart as she tried to read the expression on Eric's face.

He didn't look angry. In fact, she couldn't guess anything of what he was thinking or feeling.

"I'll call you soon," she told Abbey, and closed the phone.

The bodyguards stayed back to afford them some privacy, and though she knew Eric was accustomed to their presence, Molly felt uneasy. She knew security was necessary for all members of the royal family—and would be necessary for her child—but it was for her yet another reminder of their disparate lifestyles.

"You've decided to stay?" Eric asked politely.

She nodded.

He noted the suitcase beside her seat. "You didn't check any luggage?"

"No."

"Do you have a ticket you need to cash in?"

"No," she said again.

He sat down beside her. "Were you planning to go anywhere or did you just come here to watch the planes?"

"I thought I wanted to leave," she admitted. "But when I got here, I realized I couldn't go. Not with so much unresolved between us."

His fingertips stroked down her cheek, making her insides quiver. "Thank you."

"I'm not doing this for you—I'm doing it for our baby."

"I'm sure that's true." His smile was wry as he stood up again and offered his hand to her. "But at this point, I'll take what I can get."

Over the past couple of weeks, Molly had been to various places around the island but she still wasn't familiar enough with any of the landmarks to realize that the limo in which she was riding wasn't taking them back to the palace—until she remembered that it had taken about twenty-five minutes for Luis to get her *to* the airport and now, after forty minutes in the car, they hadn't arrived at their destination.

She looked out the window, but nothing looked familiar to her. "Where are we going?"

"To Estado de las Morales."

"Where?"

"It used to be my family's summer house on the northern coast."

"We're not staying at the palace?"

He shook his head. "We'll have more privacy at the summer house."

Privacy wasn't high on her list of priorities. She wanted—needed—other people around to run interference, to ensure that she didn't end up in Eric's bed. Again.

Because as wonderful as last night had been—and her body was still humming its agreement with *that* assessment—she knew that sex would only complicate the situation, and it was already complicated enough.

"I want us to have a chance to get to know one another," he continued. "And we can't do that with servants in every corner."

"There aren't servants at Estada des—"

"Estado de las Morales," he corrected. "There's a minimal staff to ensure things run smoothly—a housekeeper, chef and chauffeur."

Minimal staff notwithstanding, Molly knew she would have to keep the distance between her and Eric at a maximum.

"They have been at the house for a long time and can be trusted not to disclose your presence," he assured her.

"I hadn't thought about the problems that might be created for you by my decision to stay."

"It's not a problem for me but for you," he corrected. "If the paparazzi get another hint of a romance between us, you won't be able to leave the grounds without them being all over you."

She hadn't considered the potential media circus—just one more side effect of carrying a royal baby, she knew, but while she'd accepted her pregnancy and was looking forward to being a mother, the "royal" part was still a little overwhelming.

"Then we'll just have to make it clear we're just having a baby, not having a romance," she said lightly.

He smiled at her lame attempt at humor, then his attention shifted to the window when the driver made a sharp turn and he only said, "We're here."

He gave her a quick tour of the main level and introduced her to Carla, who smiled when he claimed she was "the woman who terrorizes dust bunnies," Stefan, "who will make sure you never go hungry—and that you'll never be satisfied with ordinary cuisine again," and explained that Tomas, the chauffeur/gardener/handyman had gone into town on errands but would be available if she needed a driver or pretty much anything else.

It was readily apparent to Molly that Eric had spent a lot of time at Estado de las Morales and that his relationship with the help was deeper and more personal than that of master and servant. It was yet another side of him that she hadn't seen before, an incredibly sweet and appealing side that threatened to break through all of the walls she was trying so hard to shore up.

"You would like lunch?" Stefan asked her.

Molly shook her head. "No, thanks. I'm not hungry."

She didn't need to eat—she needed time and space to figure out what she was going to do about this man who already meant far more to her than she'd ever intended for him to.

And—she stifled a yawn—about twelve hours of sleep.

"Tired?" Eric asked, as Stefan slipped back into the kitchen to give them privacy.

She nodded. "I don't think either of us got very much sleep last night."

It was a testament to how tired her brain was that she didn't manage to censor the thought before it sprang from her lips, and Eric's grin told her he knew it.

"No, I guess we didn't."

"Would it be okay…if I lie down for a while?"

"Sure." He slid his arm across her shoulders and steered her toward the staircase. "I'll take you up to your room."

"My room?"

He paused on the bottom tread and smiled at her again. "My room's beside yours, on the other side of a connecting door," he told her. "And while I can assure you I won't be locking it from my side, I'm not going to pressure you to share my bed."

"You're not?"

He chuckled. "I can't tell if that was relief or disappointment I heard in your voice."

"I'm not sure, either," she admitted, and stepped through the door he indicated.

The room wasn't as big or as fancy as the one she'd been given at the palace, but it was still pretty spectacular, with a wide window overlooking the beach that had been left open to let the scent of the sea drift in on the breeze. She was Texan born and bred and though she'd done a little traveling in recent years, she'd never ventured far from home, never yearned to settle anywhere else. But in just two weeks she'd fallen in love with this island, and as she inhaled the salty fragrance of the Mediterranean, she knew that scent would always remind her of her time in Tesoro del Mar—and of Eric.

"There's a bathroom through there," Eric said, pointing to a door on one side of the room and drawing her gaze back to him. "And my room is there." He indicated the other side.

Glancing around, she couldn't help but admire the wide, four-poster bed, the meticulously polished dressers and armoire, the cut crystal vase filled with fresh flowers. But again, it was the window that drew her, and she stepped closer to it now.

"Do you ever get used to a view like this?" she wondered.

"If you do, it takes more than thirty-six years," he told her.

She turned to him. "So that's how old you are?"

He nodded.

"I didn't want to ask—or maybe I didn't want to ask at this stage because it seemed like something I should already know."

"You can ask me whatever you want," he assured her. "I might even answer some of your questions."

She smiled at that, and he put his arms around her.

"We rushed into a lot of things," he said. "Maybe we need to slow things down a little."

"Oh. Yeah. Okay."

He chuckled again. "Honey, you're not making this easy for me."

"Nothing's been easy since you walked into my bar," she told him.

"Of all the gin joints?"

She smiled. "Something like that."

"You need to rest," he said. "And if I don't leave now, I'm not sure I'm going to."

He paused at the door and Molly's breath stalled in her lungs as she waited, wondering if he would kiss her, *wanting* him to kiss her. But he only said, "Sweet dreams," and walked away.

Eric let Molly sleep through the afternoon and tried to keep himself busy so he wouldn't think about her being alone in that big bed upstairs, so he wouldn't remember how she'd looked at him before he'd walked out the door. As if she wanted him to kiss her as much as he wanted to kiss her. But he knew that if he did, he probably wouldn't have been able to stop with one kiss—despite having promised her, not a minute earlier, that they would take things slow.

He did want to take things slow. He wanted to kiss her slowly. Then peel her clothes away slowly. Slowly run his hands over every delectable curve. And slowly sink into the wet heat of her body.

Instead, he took a quick and very cold shower.

He spent the afternoon reviewing the most recent quarterly reports of DELconnex and timeline estimates for its introduction into the European market. What had originally just been the seed of an idea that Eric had tossed out at his last meeting with the Tesorian Minister of Economic Development had quickly sprouted and taken on a life of its own. Not only was the Minister amenable to a branch of DELconnex being located on the island, he believed that branch could become the root of future expansion.

It was bigger than what Scott had proposed and, consequently, riskier. And for both of those reasons, it was also potentially much more lucrative. Eric didn't doubt that Scott would jump at the opportunity once he'd had a chance to present it to him. Except that Scott was on his honeymoon right now so the only jumping he was doing was of his wife, and that was a path Eric's mind didn't need to be traveling right now.

By four o'clock, the cold shower he'd taken hours earlier was nothing more than a distant memory, so he sent Carla upstairs to wake Molly.

She came down half an hour later, her hair still damp from the shower, her skin freshly scrubbed.

"Feel better?" he asked.

She nodded.

"Good. It's a nice night, so I've asked for dinner to be set up on the terrace, if that's okay."

She looked down at the capris and T-shirt she was wearing, then at his dark trousers paired with shirt and tie. "Am I dressed okay for dinner on the terrace?"

"You are more than okay," he told her. "You are beautiful."

"But underdressed," she guessed.

"No, I am probably overdressed."

She eyed him critically. "I don't think I've ever seen you in a pair of shorts and a T-shirt."

"A prince—or princess—is raised from birth to understand there is always the possibility of a photographer lurking around a corner, and so there are certain standards of dress that are adhered to."

She thought again of the picture that had been taken of her at the wedding, and realized he was right, and that she should learn to anticipate the same if she was going to stay on the island. But she asked, "Is that possibility one you need to worry about here?"

He shook his head. "Thankfully, no. Would you like me to see if there is a pair of shorts in my wardrobe so I can prove it to you?"

"I would be satisfied if you lost the tie."

He loosened the knot, tugged it free from the collar of his shirt. "Better?"

"Hmm." She tapped her finger on her lips, considering. Then she stepped forward and unfastened the top button, then the one below it.

"You go much further," he warned, "and I'm going to forget about dinner on the terrace to haul you back upstairs."

Molly felt her cheeks flush with color as she took a hasty step in retreat.

A quick glance at Eric revealed amusement lurking in his eyes, and something darker and edgier that she recognized as desire.

"Dinner," she reminded him. "I'm hungry."

His smile was slow and far too sexy. "So am I."

Chapter Eleven

Her cheeks flushed hotter, but she took the arm he offered and let him lead her out to the terrace.

Dinner started with a ginger carrot soup, then there was a salad of fresh greens tossed in a light vinaigrette dressing, then a blackened chicken breast served with sweet potatoes and asparagus.

"Another week of eating like this and the fact that my clothes won't fit will have nothing to do with the pregnancy," she told him.

"You don't seem to have put on much weight." His gaze skimmed over her leisurely, and she felt hot and tingly everywhere his eyes touched.

He paused at the front of her shirt, and she felt her nipples respond as immediately and obviously as if it had been a physical caress.

"Except..." His gaze lifted to hers, and there was no doubt that what she saw in his eyes now was desire. "Your breasts are fuller."

She swallowed. "Soon you won't even notice my breasts because my stomach will be sticking out so far."

"I'll still notice," he promised her.

"We didn't discuss how long we would be staying here," Molly said, not caring that it was both a desperate and obvious change of topic.

"We can stay for as long as you want."

"Don't you have royal duties or obligations to fulfill?"

"My duties are minimal," he told her. "As prince regent, Rowan bears most of the responsibility, but only until Christian is of age to assume the throne."

"Still, I hope you don't feel as if you have to entertain me for however long I'm here," she said.

"The whole point of you being here is so that we can get to know one another better," he reminded her. "And that's not going to happen if we don't spend time together."

"But we don't have to spend every single minute of every single day together."

"Are you worried that I'm going to hover—make you feel confined?"

"No," she admitted. "I just don't want you to feel as if you can't live your own life."

His lips curved, but she didn't miss the shadows that crossed his eyes. "I haven't been living my life for the past three years, why should anything change now?"

"Because you can't live the rest of your life wishing for something you can't have," she told him. "You need to figure out what you want *now.*"

"I know what I want now," he said. "And it's not very different from what I've always wanted—a family of my own. It never happened while I was in the navy—it was too hard to sustain a relationship when I was gone most of the time, but circumstances have changed. And your pregnancy has clarified that desire, because I no longer want a family in the abstract sense, I want you and our baby."

"What about love?"

He frowned at that, as if the concept was completely foreign to him.

"You say you want a family, but don't you want to fall in love first?"

"I've always thought of marriage as a duty," he admitted. "Something I needed to do for my family and my country, to ensure the continuation of the Santiago line, though that hardly seems in jeopardy with the number of babies born in the past few years."

"Is that what our baby represents to you—a legacy?"

"Our baby is everything to me."

It was the conviction in his tone that worried her more than the words. "I'm excited about becoming a parent, too, but you can't let that role define your entire existence."

"Is that what you think I'm doing?"

"I don't know," she admitted. "But since you found out that I'm pregnant, you've been so focused on this baby that I'm worried you're using it as a substitute for everything you've lost."

"I'm thrilled about being a father," he told her. "But I'm not looking to make it my full-time job."

"So what are you going to do?"

"I'm exploring some options."

"That's a rather cryptic response from a man who said I could ask whatever questions I wanted."

"I'm negotiating terms with the Minister of Economic Development to bring DELconnex here."

"You're going to work for Scott?"

"I'm going to head up the international division of the company."

"I almost forgot that Fiona told me you'd gone to MIT with Scott."

"I was also an information specialist in the navy," he told her.

"Which just reminds me how little I know about you."

Eric heard the frustration in her voice and thought he understood it. They were little more than strangers who, as a result of consequences neither had foreseen, were now tied together for the next eighteen years or more. He hoped it would be more—he wanted to believe that he and Molly could build a future and a family together. But he knew that she was wary, so he reined in his own impatience.

"We don't have to figure everything out in the first day," he told her, and she nodded her agreement.

"Although now that I've answered your questions," he said. "I have some of my own."

"What do you want to know?"

"How did your sister end up married to your fiancé?"

Molly's eyes dropped to her glass as she dragged a finger though the beads of condensation on the outside. Obviously it wasn't a question she'd expected—and probably not one she felt entirely comfortable answering. But despite her claims about wanting love, she kept her heart more heavily guarded than the royal banquet hall during a state dinner, and Eric sensed that her sister's marriage was the reason for that.

"She needed him more than I did."

"Why do I think it wasn't quite as simple as you're making it sound?"

She shrugged. "Jason is the type of guy who needs to be needed. If we ever fought, it was usually because he wanted to do something for me that I was capable of doing for myself. I didn't find out until later that he felt I was undermining his masculinity, but all I was really trying to do was assert my independence.

"Anyway, it was just after my dad died. Jason was at the

funeral home for each visitation, he stood by me at the cemetery, and he didn't understand why I couldn't cry.

"I did cry, of course, but only when I was alone. My grief was too private, too raw, to share with anyone. Jason didn't understand that.

"But Abbey fell apart," she continued her explanation. "She was devastated, although to this day I'm not sure if it was because of the depth of her grief or because she was scared to think about what his death meant for her. What would happen now? Who would take care of her?

"So Jason did. He let her cry on his shoulder and he dried her tears, and she showed her gratitude by taking him to her bed. Then he took her to Vegas and put a ring on her finger."

"At what point did they tell you what was happening?"

"Not until after the fact," she admitted. "I felt like the world's biggest dope—betrayed by both of them. But later, when I'd stopped hurting so much, I was actually kind of relieved.

"I loved Jason, but I wasn't in love with him, and if we'd actually gone through with our plans to marry, we would have made one another miserable because neither one of us could be what the other wanted or needed.

"And, until recently, Abbey and Jason were exactly that for one another. And somehow that made it easier—I could believe it wasn't a betrayal of me so much as a need to be together because they were so perfectly suited. I still believe they're a good match but they've got some pretty big obstacles to overcome if they're going to stay together."

"How is it that you believe they can make their marriage work, but you won't even give us a chance?"

"They've been married for nine years and they love one another."

"And in the nine years they've been married, have you had any serious relationships?"

"No."

"Because your ex-fiancé broke your heart?"

"Because no one I dated was interested in anything more than that."

"I find that hard to believe."

"Which is why," she continued as if he hadn't spoken, "I have to wonder what I'm even doing here."

"Giving us a chance to see that we fit."

"You know we don't. We can't. You're a prince and I'm a bartender."

"That doesn't matter."

"Of course it does," she insisted. "And now it's my turn to ask a question."

He wasn't ready to give up, but he also knew it was going to take time for Molly to see what was already obvious to him, so he only said, "What's your question?"

"What's for dessert?"

As if on cue, Carla brought in fresh fruit and custard, and while they finished up their meal, Eric accepted that he was facing an uphill battle in convincing Molly that they belonged together. Her failed engagement had proven to her that she couldn't count on anyone but herself. He intended to prove otherwise.

Molly tried to pretend that she was on vacation. She was, after all, on a beautiful island in the Mediterranean where the sun always seemed to be shining, the sand was soft and the waves inviting. But no matter how hard she tried, she couldn't relax because every minute of every day, she was conscious of Eric's presence when he was near and his absence when he wasn't.

She'd been at Estado de las Morales for nine days and, aside from that blissfully deep sleep she'd indulged in on the very first afternoon, she'd hardly slept. Every time she crawled into her bed, she was conscious of the fact that Eric was in his own bed on the other side of the adjoining door—a door that he'd assured her would not be locked from his side.

She knew the increased sexual desire she was experiencing wasn't uncommon during pregnancy. That knowledge did nothing to ease the ache inside.

But she knew what would—all she had to do was open that connecting door and walk into his room, Eric would take care of the rest. Except that it seemed they both wanted different things from each other and she worried that getting naked with him again might suggest that she wanted a more intimate relationship than she did. Because really all she wanted was sex.

Liar.

Molly sighed at the return of the nagging voice that she'd thought had been silenced by the revelation of her pregnancy to Eric.

Okay, long-term, she wanted more than sex. She wanted to fall in love with a man who could make her believe in "happily ever after." But right now her options were limited and she would happily settle for the sex.

Yeah, she was definitely suffering from hormone overload which, combined with the proximity of a very attractive man who had got her into this predicament, was an almost irresistible combination.

She heard the patio door slide open and glanced up to see Eric step out onto the deck. And her heart skipped a beat, just as it had the first time she ever saw him, just as it did every time he walked into a room.

Damn hormones.

She closed the cover on her book and set it aside.

"Dinner's going to be a little late tonight," he told her. "Stefan's in a snit."

In her short time at the summer house, she'd learned to appreciate the chef's genius and she hadn't seen any evidence that he was temperamental.

"What did you do?" she couldn't resist asking.

"Actually, *you're* the reason he is in a snit."

"Me? What did I do?"

"He had the menu planned for dinner, including oysters on the half shell with cucumber mignonette, but you are allergic to shellfish."

She had no idea what a mignonette was, but it was the second part of his statement that snagged her attention. "I don't have any food allergies."

"But raw oysters aren't recommended eating for pregnant women," he said, confirming that he'd been reading about pregnancy, too. "So it was either tell Stefan about the baby or tell him about your allergy."

She pouted. "I happen to like oysters."

"Which makes that allergy all the more unfortunate."

"So what is for dinner?"

"Well, since Stefan insisted that I—or rather you—had ruined the entire menu, I suggested that I would take you out for dinner."

"I guess that would require changing my clothes."

"That would require *wearing* some clothes," he said, his voice heavy with regret.

Molly sighed. "Couldn't we just make macaroni and cheese?"

"Macaroni and cheese?"

"I don't imagine it was a staple in the palace kitchen when you were growing up like it was in mine."

"Do you know how to make it?" he asked skeptically.

"It's not difficult."

"Then let's go see if we've got the ingredients."

The recipe Molly usually followed involved dumping the contents out of a box, and of course there was no box of prepackaged mix in Eric's kitchen. But she found some dried pasta tucked in the back of a cupboard—no doubt, Stefan usually made his fresh—and put on a pot of water to boil. While the pasta was cooking, she grated cheese for the sauce, adding a little bit of butter and milk to improve the consistency, then a little bit of flour to thicken it up.

All the while, Eric sat on the edge of the counter, watching her and asking questions about both her culinary skills and the nutritional value of the meal. She pretty much ignored him.

She dug into her bowl, humming her approval as she chewed the first mouthful.

"This is good?"

"This is very good," she told him. "And just what I wanted."

"If Stefan knew about the baby, I suspect he would cater to your every whim."

"I don't have whims."

His brows lifted. "What do you call macaroni and cheese and cookie-dough ice cream?"

She made a face. "Not two foods I would eat together, that's for sure."

"But you made me take you into town for cookie-dough ice cream last week," he reminded her.

"I didn't make you—I asked," she said. "And those are cravings, not whims."

"I stand corrected," he said, amusement dancing in his eyes. "If Stefan knew about the baby, he would indulge your cravings."

"I don't mind if you want to tell Stefan and Carla and Tomas—it's not as if we'll be able to keep it a secret much longer anyway," she told him, then grinned. "And I'm already thinking that Stefan's spicy coconut shrimp with mango salsa would be good for tomorrow."

Eric laughed and stood up to take their empty bowls to the

kitchen. When he came back, he had a leather messenger bag over his shoulder.

"Since you gave me dinner, I thought I should give something to you," he said, and handed her the bag.

"I boiled pasta and added cheese sauce, and I only fed you because you were here. It certainly wasn't a gesture that requires any payment."

"Open the bag anyway."

So she did, unfastening the straps to reveal a slim notebook computer.

"Is this for me?"

He nodded.

"Why?"

"I'm not entirely sure myself," he told her. "But when Lara found out you were staying here for a while, she suggested that you could use a computer."

She remembered the conversation she'd had with the princess in the palace gardens, and Lara's suggestion that she write down her stories. She'd never had the time before. Now she had a lot of time on her hands and no reason not to use it.

"That was very thoughtful," she said. "And generous."

"You're not going to tell me why, either?"

"Not yet." She leaned over and kissed him. "But thank you."

While Eric was busy in meetings with the Minister of Economic Development, finalizing plans to bring DELconnex to Tesoro del Mar, Molly spent a lot of time at the computer. Her typing had been slow and awkward at first, but after she'd been at it awhile, her fingers started to fly over the keyboard though they still couldn't keep up with the flow of ideas through her head.

She was just finishing up a story—one that had turned out to be a lot longer and more complicated than she'd anticipated when she wrote the opening line—when the phone rang. She expected that it would be Eric because no one else ever called, and was surprised to hear a female voice on the other end of the line.

The voice was familiar but it took her a moment to get her head out of the story before recognition—and pleasure—set in.

"Fiona?"

"If you're surprised, imagine how I felt when I stopped in at Shea's to see my best friend after I got back from my honeymoon only to find that she'd left the restaurant under the questionable management of her sister to shack up with a prince."

Molly picked her way carefully through the land mines that were planted throughout Fiona's words and asked, "How was the honeymoon?"

"It was incredible," Fiona admitted. "But that wasn't the part of my statement that I wanted you to focus on."

"And I did *not* leave Abbey in charge of the restaurant—I left Karen in charge of the restaurant. Jason is the new night manager and Abbey is only working there part-time."

"Which is definitely a topic worthy of conversation at another time. Right now, I want to hear about whatever happened between you and Eric to have you moving in with him."

"It's only a temporary arrangement," Molly insisted.

"Okay—but why? Not that I'm not thrilled," Fiona hastened to assure her. "I think Eric is great, but whenever I even tried to mention his name to you, you insisted that you weren't looking to get involved."

"I wasn't. I couldn't." She blew out a breath. "Do you remember me telling you about the guy I met at the bar?"

"How could I forget?" Fiona teased. "It's not every day that you have that kind of reaction to— Oh. My. God. It was *Eric*."

That was the thing about Fiona—give her enough dots, and it usually didn't take her too long to connect them.

"It was Eric," she agreed. "But at the time, I didn't know that you knew him. Then when we met again at your ranch, I was too embarrassed to admit that I knew him because I was afraid you would know he was the one."

"But now you've picked up where you left off?" Fiona asked hopefully.

"It's a little more complicated than that. A lot more complicated, actually." She hesitated. "Fiona, I'm pregnant."

"What?"

"You heard me."

"Oh. My. God."

"Yeah," Molly said.

"When are you due?"

"Early January."

"What was Eric's reaction?"

So Molly spent a few minutes filling her cousin in on all of the details of everything that had transpired since Eric had learned of her pregnancy.

"I'll bet he asked you to marry him," Fiona guessed, since Molly had opted to leave that part out.

"I'm not going to."

"Why not?"

"I can't believe you even need to ask me that question."

"He's a prince. He's the father of your baby. And you obviously have great chemistry together."

"And you think that's enough to base a marriage on?"

"There are plenty of marriages based on less," Fiona told her. Then another thought occurred to her and she asked, "Does Abbey know?"

"No." She knew no further explanation was required.

"Grandma and Grandpa?"

"No," she said again.

"Well, I'm glad I'm not the last to know," Fiona said philosophically. "But unless you're planning to stay in Tesoro del Mar forever, you're going to have to tell them."

"I know," Molly admitted.

"So when are you planning to come home?"

"We haven't really talked about that."

"Too busy playing…house?" her cousin teased.

Molly had to laugh. "I've missed you, Fee."

"Me, too. But whatever you decide about marrying Eric—"

"I already told you what I decided."

"—you will come back for my rescheduled wedding reception in October, won't you?"

"Of course," Molly assured her.

She talked to her cousin for a few more minutes and, when she finally hung up the phone, knew she couldn't delay sharing the news with the rest of her family any longer. But she dialed her grandparents' number first.

In the five weeks that Molly had been in Tesoro del Mar, Abbey had usually been the one to initiate telephone contact so she was understandably surprised to hear from her sister now.

It had never been as easy for Molly to talk to Abbey as it was to talk to Fiona. She sometimes wondered if Abbey might not have turned to Jason for comfort after their father's death if Molly had been able to offer the support she'd needed. And while that was water long under the bridge, it certainly hadn't helped the relationship between the sisters.

They made small talk for a few minutes—mostly about the restaurant—but Molly knew the longer she waited the harder it would be, so she finally said, "I called because I have something to tell you."

"News about the hunky prince?" her sister asked.

"Yeah. Kind of."

"So tell," Abbey urged.

Which sounded simple enough, but still the words stuck in her throat. "Well, actually…Eric and I…we…or rather I'm…pregnant."

There was, for half a minute, complete silence on the other end of the line.

Then Abbey gave a short, breathless laugh. "I'm sorry," she said. "The line must have cut out because for a second, I actually thought you said you were pregnant."

"I did," she said softly. "I am."

She heard the sharp intake of breath, and hated knowing that she'd caused her sister pain.

"Pregnant," Abbey said again, the word little more than an agonized whisper that reflected the heartache and disappointment of so many failed attempts to have a child of her own.

"I thought you should hear it from me," Molly said gently.

But neither her tone nor her words consoled her sister.

"When you told me you were staying in Tesoro del Mar," Abbey said, "I figured you were having a fling with Eric, but I didn't expect it was anything more than that. And you probably knew you couldn't hold on to him for very long—you couldn't even hold on to Jason—so you got pregnant. And now Eric will probably feel compelled to marry you and everything will be just perfect."

Molly knew her sister was lashing out because she was hurting so badly, so she was prepared to let her vent. But all she heard after that was a click and a dial tone.

Eric hadn't intended to eavesdrop on Molly's conversation, but he'd been walking past the den when he heard her voice and he'd peeked around the corner just to give a quick wave and let her know he was home. She didn't see him—but what he saw stopped him in his tracks.

She was crying.

Her eyes were drenched with moisture and pain and silent tears tracked slowly down her cheeks. He'd never seen her cry, and the sight of those tears now cut him off at the knees.

He didn't hear her say goodbye, but her hand trembled as she placed the receiver back in the cradle, and somehow he knew.

"Your sister," he guessed.

She nodded and wiped her hands over her cheeks, as if to hide the evidence of her tears.

He pushed back her chair and lifted her into his arms.

Her eyes widened, but she held on as he carried her to the sofa, sitting down to cuddle her in his lap.

"Just let me hold you for a minute," he said.

And she did. She buried her face in his shirt and she cried until there were no more tears inside.

He rubbed his hand over her back and murmured soft, soothing words as he remembered the conversation they'd had just a couple weeks earlier when she'd told him she'd never cried on her ex-fiancé's shoulder. He wasn't sure if it was a testament to how close they'd grown over the past couple of months that she'd let her guard down enough to accept comfort from him now or if he'd just caught her at a weak moment, but he was glad that he'd been there when she'd obviously needed someone.

"I had to tell her," Molly said softly.

"Of course you did."

"I talked to Fiona earlier, and I told her. And she was so excited for us. I knew Abbey wouldn't be happy—I know why she couldn't be—but I didn't want to hurt her."

"I know."

"Fiona and Scott have rescheduled their wedding reception for next month and, of course, she wants us to be there, and I couldn't just show up without giving Abbey—or my grandparents—warning."

"Does this mean I'll get to meet your grandparents?" he asked, deliberately shifting the focus of the conversation so she wouldn't start crying again.

"Do you want to meet them?"

"Of course."

"They know you're the father of my baby," she warned him.

"Then it might be a good idea to introduce me to them as your fiancé," he suggested.

"Except that we're not engaged."

"We could be."

She sighed and pulled away from him. "Why can't you let this go?"

"Because you're using one bad relationship experience as an excuse to avoid marrying me."

"You don't know what you're talking about."

"I know that you've got legitimate reasons for thinking twice before making a commitment—"

"I'm not opposed to marriage," she interjected. "Just marriage to you."

"What's wrong with me?" he demanded.

"I don't think you really want me to answer that question."

"Actually, I do."

She frowned. "You want me to make a list of all of your character flaws?"

"Let's just stick to the ones that are relevant to your not wanting to marry me."

"Okay—you're sarcastic."

His brows rose. "*I'm* sarcastic?"

"You're demanding."

"I have high expectations," he admitted.

"You're stubborn."

"Because I don't give up when something matters?"

"You think you have an answer for everything."

"I like to consider all possible solutions to a problem."

"You're arrogant—you expect to get what you want when you want it."

"I go after what I want," he clarified.

"You're a prince."

"Why is that a reason to not marry me?"

"Because I don't want my child living his or her life under constant media scrutiny."

"You've met all of my nieces and nephews," he pointed out. "Did you get the impression that any one of them has been scarred as a result of the media attention?"

"Two of them are still in diapers."

"Then I guess there's still hope that your completely irrational argument might someday prove to be valid."

"There's that sarcasm again," she noted.

"And you say I'm stubborn," he muttered.

"Shall I go on?"

"I'd say the only legitimate reason you might have for turning down my proposal is my state of mind—because you, Molly Shea, are driving me crazy."

She could hear the frustration in his tone. Should have known to back down. Instead she said, "By all means, let's add questionable mental health to the list."

And pushed him too far.

He responded by hauling her into his arms and kissing her.

Chapter Twelve

She should have been furious. Instead, she melted into his embrace.

He coaxed her lips apart; she opened for him willingly. Their tongues met, mated. Desire pumped through her system like a drug, making her skin burn, her head spin, her heart pound.

With equal parts determination and regret, she tore her mouth from his and dropped her head to his chest. His heart was racing as fast as hers, his breathing was just as ragged.

"And that's another reason I can't marry you."

"You don't like the way I kiss?"

"You'll do anything to get what you want," she corrected. "And you know I can't think when you kiss me like that."

"I don't want you to think," he said, stroking a hand down her back. "Because then you're conjuring up reasons why we shouldn't be together when it's obvious to me that we should."

"You're a prince," she said again. "And I'm a bartender."

"I'm a man and you're a woman, and we're good together, Molly. You know we are. So what is it that you're really afraid of?"

Falling in love with you.

But she didn't tell him that, of course. If he had the slightest clue about her growing feelings for him, he would find a way to manipulate them to his advantage and she'd find herself walking down the aisle. And she refused to let that happen.

But her emotions were already involved—far more than she was willing to admit to, even to herself. Because she'd started to fall in love with him right from the start, and she'd continued falling ever since. Even when he frustrated and annoyed her, she couldn't seem to stop it from happening, and she knew it was only a matter of time before she hit the ground with a splat.

He talked to her and he listened to her as if he really cared about what she was saying. He made her laugh and he looked at her as if she was the only woman in the world who mattered. And when he kissed her, he made the rest of the world disappear.

She knew that if he made a promise to her, he wouldn't break it. That was the kind of man he was—honest, sincere, steadfast and reliable. The kind of man a woman couldn't help but fall in love with.

But would he ever love her? That was the question that continued to hold her back. It wasn't enough that he was an honorable man, intent on marrying the mother of his child because he believed it was the right thing to do. Emotions, at least so far as he was concerned, didn't really enter into it. And if he could never feel about her the way she felt about him, it would break her heart.

Molly didn't answer his question, but Eric hadn't really expected that she would. Besides, he had a pretty good idea what she was afraid of—getting in too deep, caring too much. Yeah,

Abbey and Jason had really done a number on her, and he didn't blame her for being reluctant to trust anyone else.

And though it frustrated him to think about how little progress they'd made with respect to their relationship in the month and a half that they'd been together at the summer house, he reminded himself every day that they were making progress. The fact that she was still here proved it.

Even more telling, he thought, was that she'd made no mention in recent weeks of going back to Texas and he was beginning to hope that she might someday think of Tesoro del Mar as home. A few months ago, that thought might have surprised him, but now he was a lot more certain about what he wanted.

He'd known Molly only a few months, but he almost couldn't remember what his life had been like before he'd met her, and he sure didn't want to imagine his life without her in it—and only partly because she was carrying his child.

He wanted the baby, no doubt about that. And, if not for the child, he probably wouldn't be thinking in terms of marriage, certainly not this early on in their relationship. But even if she wasn't pregnant, he knew now that he would still want Molly.

"Okay," he said at last. "I won't push. I know how to be patient when the situation warrants it."

Her brows lifted. "So now I'm a situation?"

His lips quirked. "No, you're a source of extreme frustration. Night after night, for the past six weeks, I've been lying awake in my bed, unable to stop thinking about you."

"Thinking about sex," she corrected.

"Thinking about *you,*" he said again. "And I think it's interesting how every time I get a little too close—and not just physically—you withdraw."

"Maybe I don't like you."

He smiled at that. "That's one possibility," he allowed. "Another is that you *do* like me. Maybe more than you want to. And maybe living in close quarters and not sharing a bed is starting to drive you crazy, too."

She eyed him warily. "You're not honestly suggesting that we should have sex to dissipate some of this tension?"

"No, I don't think this tension is going to dissipate. I think this tension is proof of the chemistry that has been there from the start and an attraction that has only strengthened and deepened over the past few months." He smiled again. "But if *you* want to believe it, if that's what will finally convince you to open the damn door between our bedrooms, I'll go along with it."

"A man will go along with anything if it will get a woman naked," she said, but without any real heat.

"That might be true," he acknowledged. "But this isn't about a man and a woman—it's about me and you. And it turns out you're the only woman for me, the woman I think I might be falling in love with."

There was a long silence. Then Molly spoke. "So are you going to talk this to death or are you going to take me to bed?"

Four weeks after Molly had raced him to his bed, the chemistry between them hadn't even begun to fizzle. And as phenomenal as their lovemaking was, what Eric really cherished was the growing closeness with Molly. They were talking, communicating, sharing their hopes and dreams for their child and the future.

She'd been seeing a local obstetrician who allowed them to sneak in through a back door directly into an examining room so that they could avoid being recognized by other patients. They had told no one outside of their immediate families and the servants at Estado de las Morales of her pregnancy, but Molly knew it was only a matter of time before someone somewhere figured it out, so she was enjoying the relative anonymity and privacy while it lasted. And so far, everything was progressing well and on schedule with the baby. Just a few days earlier, she'd had a twenty-week ultrasound that indicated the baby was a girl, so they'd started using *"she"* and *"her"* in reference to the child, and he found that somehow made the baby seem even more real. Of course, the expansion of her waistline was another reminder.

He marveled at the changes in her body and couldn't help but smile every time he felt the tiniest movement of their baby in her womb. The only real source of friction in their relationship was Molly's continuing refusal to marry him. Although she claimed the friction was caused by his refusal to accept her unwillingness to marry him.

"I really think we should schedule our wedding soon to ensure it happens before the baby is born," he suggested for the thousandth time.

"You don't want to marry me," Molly said for the thousandth time. "You want to marry the mother of your child, to ensure her legitimacy and secure her status as your heir. I just happen to be the woman you got pregnant."

"And the woman currently in my bed," he pointed out.

"Keep pushing and you'll push me out of it," she warned.

He responded by tightening his arms around her, and she sighed and relaxed against him.

"Lara told me that Rowan was worried that the people of Tesoro del Mar would be scandalized by his relationship with the royal nanny. Can you imagine how they'd react if they knew you were involved with an American bartender?"

"Neither your nationality nor your occupation are as important as the fact that you're carrying my child."

"My mother ran out on her family, my father liked to drink a little too much and I was once engaged to my sister's husband."

"None of that matters to me."

"It should."

He took her hands. "You are a warm and beautiful woman. You're kind and compassionate and—"

"And you're a prince," she reminded him. "You could have any woman you want."

"I want you," he said simply.

She sighed. "Why are you being so difficult about this?"

"I think the determination of which one of us is being difficult is a matter of perspective."

Her lips curved at that. "Maybe it is. But the fact remains that we've been going around in circles about this issue for weeks now."

"And we'll continue to do so until you agree to marry me and give our baby the family she deserves."

Molly was quiet for a moment. "A long time ago, when I was still young and naive enough to believe in 'happily ever afters,' I expected that I would be married before I ever had a baby. I wanted my children to be born into a traditional family. But even if we married, nothing about our life would be traditional, nothing about our child's life would be normal because she will be royal."

"The child will be royal whether or not we marry," he pointed out. "And I happen to think my family is pretty wonderful despite being royal."

"They are wonderful," she agreed. "But I don't see Rowan picking up pizza on his way home after work or Lara carpooling with other moms at the day care or other normal family-type activities."

"Normal is a matter of interpretation," he insisted.

And another circle was complete without them getting any closer to setting a wedding date.

* * *

The argument with Eric was still on her mind several hours later, so Molly was pleased when Lara stopped by, granting her a reprieve from her own thoughts.

"I had a few hours free and decided to check in and see how your collection of children's stories was coming along."

"It keeps growing," Molly admitted. "Every time I think it's the last one, another one pops into my mind."

"How many do you have so far?"

"Fourteen."

"Wow." Lara laughed. "That's a lot more than I would have guessed."

"Me, too." She smiled at Carla as she brought in a tray of tea and cookies. "Thanks."

"What are you going to do with them now?" Lara asked, accepting the cup of tea that Molly poured for her.

"Lexi's drawing me some pictures to go with the magic frog story so I can have it printed and bound for Matthew."

"He'll love it," Lara assured her. "But I was actually wondering about your plans on a bigger scale."

"I don't have any bigger plans."

"Well, you should start making some because I have a friend—he's a friend of a friend, actually—who wants to see what you've got."

"Someone wants to read my stories?"

Lara smiled. "He's not just 'someone.' He's an editor at a major publishing house in England."

Molly bobbled her cup and had to set it aside for fear she would drop it. "An editor?"

"Did I overstep?" Lara asked cautiously.

"No. I'm just… An editor… I'm stunned. I can't believe it."

Lara grinned. "Good. And while you're basking in that little revelation, I'm going to risk overstepping again and ask you when the heck you're going to put my brother-in-law out of his misery by agreeing to marry him."

Molly sighed. "I can't believe you're taking his side on this."

"It's not about sides," Lara denied. "And if you think I can't understand how difficult this is for you, you're wrong, because I've been exactly where you are."

"Where is it that you think I am?" Molly asked cautiously.

"Involved with a man who seems completely wrong for you."

She didn't bother to deny her feelings. "I'd say the problem is more that I'm completely wrong for him."

"And yet, anyone who knows Eric and has seen the way he looks at you, would dispute that."

"He's attracted to me." She glanced down at her swollen belly. "Or he was, at one time, obviously."

Lara laughed. "I don't think the attraction has faded. If anything, I would guess that Eric's feelings for you have grown and deepened over the past few months, and not just because you're carrying his child."

"None of which changes the fact that I'm wrong for him."

"Isn't that his decision to make?" the princess asked gently.

"Maybe. Except that he's so determined to do the right thing—which he insists is marrying me—that I'm not sure he's considered the long-term consequences."

"And why are you so determined *not* to marry him? What are you afraid of?" Lara echoed the question her brother-in-law had asked the day before. "That you'll fall in love with him? Or that you won't?"

And Molly found herself admitting to Lara a truth that she was only starting to acknowledge herself. "I'm afraid that I already have."

* * *

Molly had never been a nervous flier. Of course, she could count on one hand the number of times she'd been on an airplane, and there was always so much excitement associated with whatever journey she'd been about to embark on that she hadn't worried about any of the details. But as she stood at the security counter and watched the minutes tick away on the clock on the wall, she was definitely starting to worry.

She tucked her hands into her pockets and noted the steady progression of travelers moving through the other lines. Families with children, couples, singles. No one seemed to be subject to anything more than the standard questions and a minimal wait. Why were they concerned about her?

Because she knew there was some concern. When she'd first walked up to the security gate, the guard had asked about her destination and the purpose of her trip in a bored tone that told her he'd asked the exact same questions too many times before. Then he'd scanned her passport and frowned at the computer screen.

"Is there a problem?" she'd asked, confident that there couldn't be. It was the same passport she'd used to enter the country and it didn't expire for another two years.

But the response didn't reassure her. "Wait one minute, please."

Then the guard had left her standing there while he took her passport through a secured, frosted-glass door marked *SEGURIDAD/SÉCURITÉ.*

And she'd been standing and waiting a lot longer than "one minute."

Maybe she should have waited for Eric to return from his business trip so she could fly to San Antonio with him, but after her recent conversation with Fiona, she'd been anxious to get home and see her family. Eric had agreed to meet her in Texas and they would fly back together again after the weekend.

She looked at the clock again, calculated that he'd been gone at least seven minutes, and was grateful that she still had almost an hour before her flight was scheduled to leave. Whatever was going on, she was sure it would be straightened out in time for her to get on the plane.

Her certainty wavered when the same guard stepped out of the office again—followed by three other men. Two were some kind of military, evidenced by their uniforms and the weapons they carried, the third was wearing a suit with a badge clipped on the jacket pocket and an air of authority that made her pulse race.

She'd done nothing wrong. Logically, she knew there was no reason for them to detain her. But the escalating fear was a lot stronger than logic at the moment.

"Miss Shea?" the man in the suit said.

She swallowed, her heart pounding so hard she wondered that he couldn't hear it. "Yes?"

"I'm Aidan Lamontagne, Chief of Airport Security. Would you come into my office for a minute, please?"

She knew it wasn't a question so much as a directive. She nodded anyway and murmured her agreement.

"Is there a problem?" she asked again, not quite certain any more and all too conscious of the military guards posted on either side of the door, no doubt to prevent any attempted escape.

"That's what we're trying to figure out," he admitted. "You're an American citizen, Miss Shea?"

"Yes."

"And you've been in Tesoro del Mar since May twenty-ninth?"

She shifted in her chair and wondered if it was the extension of her visit that was the problem. Though she'd come into the country on the royal family's private plane, she'd still filled out immigration papers indicating her intended date of departure—a date that had passed more than two months earlier.

"Yes," she said again.

"For business or pleasure?"

She shifted in her chair again. "I came for a friend's wedding."

"When is the wedding?"

"It was June tenth."

"And since then?" he prompted.

"I've been on something of an extended vacation."

"Where are you staying?"

"With a friend." She folded her hands in her lap. "I'm not sure I understand the reason for all of these questions."

"The address where you're staying, Miss Shea," he prompted in the same implacable tone.

"3880 Camino Del norte De la Costa."

She saw recognition light in his eyes, knew he was familiar with the address, as no doubt someone employed with national security would be familiar with all of the royal family's properties.

"You are staying at Estado de las Morales?"

She nodded. "Yes."

"As a guest of the royal family?"

"Yes." She felt her cheeks heat up in response to his narrowed gaze. She and Eric had both wanted to ensure her presence at the estate wasn't common knowledge because they wanted time to let their relationship develop without public scrutiny. Now, with this security officer so obviously skeptical about her connection to the royal family, she wondered if that had been a mistake.

"I'm a—" she swallowed "—a friend of Prince Eric Santiago."

"You are aware that His Royal Highness is currently out of the country."

"Of course I am," she said wearily. "He's in Monaco on business. He's scheduled to return on Thursday and was planning to meet me in Texas for my grandparents' anniversary."

He pushed his chair away from the desk. "Excuse me a moment, please."

He walked past the guards and into the outer office. She saw the light on his phone illuminate, confirming that he'd left her to make a private call.

She brushed her hands over the thighs of her jeans, more annoyed than worried now. Obviously there had been some kind of mistake—she just hoped Mr. Lamontagne would clear it up so she could get on the plane. Over the past few months, she'd been too preoccupied trying to figure out her relationship with Eric and making plans for the future of their child to think much about everything—and everyone—she'd left behind in Texas. But since Fiona had contacted her about coming home, she'd been thinking about home a lot.

She knew her cousin didn't need her help with anything so much as she wanted all the details of what was happening with Eric, and though Molly was looking forward to spending time with Fiona, she didn't know how she was going to answer her questions. Because the fact was, almost four months after moving in with Eric, she didn't have any more answers about her future than she did on day one. While there was no doubt they both wanted what was best for their child, they couldn't seem to agree on what that was.

Or maybe it was her own feelings for the prince that were confusing the issue.

Mr. Lamontagne's return pushed these thoughts from her mind and she gave him her full attention, anxious to know the reason she'd been detained and that it had been cleared up.

"I apologize for the confusion," he said, "and can advise that the palace is sending someone to pick you up."

"Pick me up?"

He nodded.

"But I'll miss my flight." She glanced at her watch. "I'm supposed to be on a plane to the United States in twenty minutes."

"I'm sorry, Miss Shea."

That was it—no other explanation was given.

She wanted to kick and scream but she knew it would be no use. He was just doing his job.

"Officer Melas will escort you to the administration area on the second floor to wait for your party there."

Eric was on his way home from Monaco when Rowan contacted him about the incident with Molly at the airport.

"You need to fix this," he said.

"I'll track down Lamontagne as soon as we land."

"I meant that you need to fix this with Molly," Rowan said, confirming that he knew Eric was responsible for what had happened.

And Eric knew that Molly would be more difficult to deal with than the security officer.

He'd made a lot of mistakes in his life, but he was hard-pressed to find one that could top this. Molly was going to be furious when she realized he was responsible for flagging her passport so she couldn't leave the country without him knowing, and he couldn't blame her. His actions had been uncharacteristically impulsive and shortsighted, and he had no doubt he would pay for them now.

She was in the conservatory when he got home, surrounded by flowers and plants and illuminated by the sunlight streaming through the windows. Her computer was perched on her knees and her fingers raced across the keyboard. After a few minutes, she paused and lifted a hand to rub her belly.

"Writer's block or baby kicks?" he asked.

She looked up at him and smiled. "Hi. I didn't think you were coming back until tomorrow."

He crossed the room to give her a long, lingering kiss. "The meetings finished up early and I was missing you."

"But I wasn't supposed to be here," she reminded him.

"I know. I stopped by the security office to see Aidan Lamontagne and straightened that out before I came home."

"So it's fixed?" She set aside her computer and stood up. "You have a quick conversation with the head of airport security, who wouldn't let me on an airplane twelve hours ago, and he's suddenly reassured that I'm not a threat to national security?"

He'd thought she would be pleased that the problem was sorted out. He hadn't anticipated that she'd be suspicious by the ease with which he'd done so.

"If he'd ever believed you were, you would have left the airport in handcuffs."

"Well, I guess I should be grateful for that—but I'd still like to know why I was detained."

And she had a right to know.

Bracing himself for her reaction, he admitted, "You came up on the system as a person of interest with a directive to contact the palace if you attempted to leave the country."

"What? Why?"

"Because I was pissed when I woke up the morning after Scott and Fiona's wedding and found you were gone."

She stared at him, stunned, hurt. "*You* arranged it so I couldn't leave the country? You asked me to stay—you made me think that I had a choice, but I never really did. You were never going to let me leave."

"I wasn't going to let you leave without talking to me about why and where you were planning to go."

"Neither one of those questions should have been a big mystery to you. I was leaving because the wedding was over and I was going home."

"Okay—maybe I overreacted."

"Maybe?" The hurt had quickly turned to fury.

"I did overreact," he admitted. "I just didn't want you going anywhere until we'd had a chance to talk."

"Haven't we done enough talking over the past four months?" The ice in her tone chilled him to the bone.

"I forgot that I'd had your passport flagged."

She looked away, but not before he saw that her eyes had filled with tears. "I hate this."

"I said I was sorry," he told her. "What more can I do?"

"I'm sure you are sorry," she agreed. "Though I'm not sure if you're sorry that you ever did it or just sorry that you forgot to undo it before you got caught. But what I hate is that you have that kind of power. What's going to happen if we disagree on an issue about our child? Am I going to have any say or is everything just going to be your way because you can make it so?"

He was grateful that the chirp of his cell sounded before he could open his mouth, because he had no idea what he could say to diffuse an explosive situation that he knew was entirely of his own making.

He flipped it open, but kept his eyes on Molly. "Yes?"

She'd turned her back to him and folded her arms across her chest in a classically defensive posture. He wanted to take her in his arms, to soothe the hurt even though he knew he'd caused it.

He listened to the voice on the phone, then snapped it shut again and told her, "The plane is ready."

She closed the lid on her computer, tucked it under her arm. "This doesn't make everything okay."

Eric sighed wearily as he watched her storm out of the room—knowing and regretting that it was true.

Chapter Thirteen

Molly's mood hadn't improved much by the time they landed in San Antonio. She was still stunned by the revelation of what Eric had done, and furious there was nowhere she could go to get away from him.

A few months earlier, Molly had agreed to sublet her apartment above the restaurant to a new waitress, so she'd planned to stay with her grandparents to maximize her time with them. When Eric first told her he wanted to stay with her, she'd been pleased by his interest in spending time with her family. Now she had to wonder—did he really want to meet her grandparents, or did he just want to stick close to keep an eye on her?

She'd honestly believed they'd grown close over the past few months, but now Molly wondered if she really knew him at all.

As he drove the rental car through the familiar streets of town, she was both excited and nervous about the reunion with her grandparents. Molly had spoken to them regularly over the past several months, but after telling them about her pregnancy—an announcement which had been met, not unexpectedly, with a lecture about "the lack of morals in young people these days"—she'd been careful to steer clear of that topic in subsequent conversations.

There would be no steering clear of it this weekend, she knew. Not when the proof of it was now obvious to even an octogenarian with bifocals.

But her grandmother made no comment about the belly that pressed between them when she greeted her at the door with a warm hug.

"I'm so glad you're finally here," Theresa Shea said, kissing both of Molly's cheeks. "And look at you—you're glowing."

"I'm hot, Grandma. Hauling around an extra twenty pounds has thrown off my internal thermostat."

"Nonsense," Theresa chided, turning her attention from her disgruntled granddaughter to the man standing in the doorway behind her. "And you must be Molly's prince."

"Please, just call me Eric," he said.

"Hmm," she said, which Molly knew meant she was reserving judgment. Ordinarily, the presence of royalty would have flustered her grandmother, but she knew Eric's status was tempered in Theresa's mind by the fact that he'd impregnated her granddaughter. "You got any luggage? I can call Lawrence to get it for you."

"Just these," he said, indicating the two small suitcases in his hands.

"Molly's can go upstairs, the first door on the right. You'll be sleeping on the pull-out downstairs."

If Eric was surprised by the sleeping arrangements, he didn't show it and left his bag at the entrance as he took hers up the stairs.

"Where is Grandpa?" Molly asked.

"In the garage, tinkering with some kind of engine with the Walters' boy."

For as long as Molly could remember, her grandfather had always been tinkering with one thing or another. "I'll go out and say hi," she said. After which, she wanted only to kick off her shoes, put her feet up and relax.

"You can say hi later," Theresa told her. "I want to go shopping."

"Shopping?" Molly asked wearily.

"I need a new outfit for the party."

Molly stared at her grandmother. "For Fiona and Scott's wedding celebration?"

Theresa nodded.

"But—it's tomorrow."

"I know that," her grandmother said with just the slightest hint of irritation. "I might be old, but I'm not senile."

So instead of putting her feet up, Molly put a smile on her face and took her grandmother shopping.

Four hours later and still empty-handed, Theresa announced that she'd had enough of the crowds at the mall and was certain she could find something in her closet at home that was appropriate.

But when they passed a little coffee shop, her grandmother steered her inside. "I want a cup of tea," she explained.

"We can have tea at your house," Molly said.

"Yes, but we can't talk with your young man around."

"He's not my young man."

"Which is what we need to talk about."

So it was that Molly was sitting across from her at a little table with a cup of decaf in her hand.

"He should marry you," her grandmother said firmly.

Molly stared into her cup, well aware that the admission she had to make was going to swing the direction of her grandmother's wrath, but knowing she had no choice. If her grandmother started in on Eric about the importance of their child being born legitimate—as, given thirty seconds alone with him, she just might do—he would undoubtedly admit that Molly was the one holding out.

"He thinks so, too," she admitted.

Theresa's cup clattered against her saucer. "He asked you to marry him?"

"It wasn't actually a proposal," Molly said.

"But he wants to do the right thing?"

Molly sighed. "Who says it's the right thing? Why is having a child out of wedlock more scandalous than entering into a marriage for all of the wrong reasons?"

"Giving your baby a family isn't a wrong reason."

"It didn't work for my parents, did it?"

Theresa sighed. "Because your parents weren't willing to work at their marriage."

"Because they both felt trapped by circumstances."

"Is that how you feel?" her grandmother demanded. "Because I might be old-fashioned in a lot of ways, but I know darn well that a young woman who gets pregnant nowadays only stays that way if she wants her baby."

"I do want my baby," she admitted, her hand automatically moving to her rounded belly. "But I'm not sure I would ever have seen Eric again if not for the connection with Fiona and Scott, and even now, I'm not sure he wants to be a husband and a father so much as he feels compelled to do the right thing."

"Wanting to do the right thing proves the boy was raised right," Theresa said approvingly.

Molly couldn't help but smile. "The 'boy' is thirty-six years old and seventh in line to the throne of his country."

Theresa's gaze sharpened. "Is *that* what's bothering you—that he's a prince?"

"We have nothing in common, Grandma. A marriage between us would be doomed to fail even before it began."

"If you have nothing in common, the last four months must have been extremely difficult for you."

Molly felt her cheeks flush. "Okay—so maybe we're not completely incompatible," she admitted.

"Then maybe you need to consider that marrying him isn't a completely unreasonable idea."

Eric was sleeping on a lumpy couch in Molly's grandparents' basement. Correction: he was *trying* to sleep on a lumpy couch in Molly's grandparents' basement, a fact which might have made him smile if he wasn't so damn uncomfortable.

They obviously knew he and Molly had been intimate—she wouldn't be pregnant otherwise. And he knew that their acceptance of the baby she carried didn't translate into approval of that fact.

He also understood that the lumpy couch was punishment for sleeping with their granddaughter outside of the sanctity of marriage. And now that he was on the verge of becoming a father of a baby girl himself, he appreciated that position because there was no way his little girl was going to be unchaperoned with a man until he was her husband.

He didn't sleep well—and while the bed was partly to blame, the recent strain in his relationship with Molly was the bigger problem. He knew it was his own fault; he just didn't know how to fix it.

He felt a little bit better after a breakfast of eggs and bacon and fried potatoes and freshly squeezed juice. It wasn't a fancy meal but it was hot and hearty. The only thing he missed at the table was Molly.

"Is Molly still sleeping?" he finally asked.

Theresa chuckled. "Goodness, no. She was up and gone more than an hour ago. Took some of my homemade cinnamon rolls over to Abbey at the restaurant."

Probably to avoid having breakfast with him, he couldn't help but think, again regretting the distance between them. Had he not bungled things so badly, she might have asked him to go with her, because he guessed that she could use some moral support in facing her sister.

"How is Abbey doing?" he asked cautiously.

"Are you asking if she's accepted that Molly's going to have a baby?"

He nodded.

"She's getting there. It probably wouldn't have come as such a shock if Molly had been married first. That's the usual order of things—wedding and then baby—and a ceremony might have prepared Abbey for the possibility that her sister was going to be a mother."

"Do you really think so?" he asked. "Or is that just your way of asking about my intentions regarding your granddaughter."

"I really think so," she said. "Besides, Molly already told me that you asked her to marry you."

"She did?"

"Thought she'd enjoy watching you on the hot seat, didn't you?"

"Yeah," he admitted, knowing he deserved to be there.

"I love my granddaughter," Theresa said now. "But she's too stubborn for her own good sometimes."

"I can be just as stubborn," he promised her.

She smiled. "I'm counting on that."

Molly's apprehension increased with every mile that brought her closer to Shea's. This would be the first time she'd seen her sister since she'd left San Antonio almost five months earlier and since the conversation in which she'd told Abbey of her pregnancy. Which was why Molly had a box of Grandma's homemade cinnamon buns and jittery nerves as she walked across the parking lot early Friday morning.

She'd thought about asking Eric to go with her. Despite everything that had happened in the last twenty-four hours, she trusted that he would be there for her if she needed him. But Molly wouldn't let herself need him.

The door was unlocked, so she tucked her key back in her pocket and walked in. She set the box of pastries on the counter. "Got any coffee to go with these?"

"Molly!" Abbey's eyes lit up and she immediately came around the bar to embrace her sister.

It was a warmer greeting than Molly had expected. And then they hugged, and Abbey's gaze dropped to her sister's belly and her eyes filled with tears.

Molly held her breath.

"You look good," Abbey said, then smiled at her sister through her tears. "Really good, Molly."

She swallowed. "Thanks."

Abbey moved back to the other side of the bar. "You said something about coffee?"

"Yeah, that would be great. Make mine decaf."

Abbey poured two cups, pushed one across the bar.

Molly slid onto a stool. "Was it really only a few months ago that we were on opposite sides of this counter?"

"Hard to believe isn't it?" Abbey folded her arms on the polished wood. "I'm really glad you came in. I was going to call you, but when I realized you were coming home for Fiona and Scott's reception, I decided it would be better to talk to you in person—to thank you in person."

"Thank me?"

"To apologize *and* to thank you," her sister clarified. "I was kind of nasty to you the last time we spoke."

"I understand why you were upset."

"I *was* upset. And hurt and frustrated and angry. It just seemed so unfair that Jason and I have been trying so hard for so long to have a baby and you spend one night with a guy and end up pregnant."

Molly only nodded.

"And then, I was telling Jason about it—" she managed a smile "—okay, I was complaining to Jason about how unfair it was, and how your baby should have been our baby, and I finally accepted that wanting a child doesn't mean I need to have a baby. There are tons of babies out there in need of families and maybe Jason and I could be that family to one or more of them."

She paused to take a breath and to blink away the moisture from her eyes. "We have an appointment with a couple of adoption agencies next week and another with a caseworker from Family Services. We know it might take a while before we get a child of our own but there are a lot of kids who need a temporary home so we thought we might foster while the adoption process gets underway. Or maybe we could even adopt through Family Services—I didn't realize that could be done but I was talking to Karen about fostering and she told me that was how her sister adopted both of her kids."

As the story spilled out, her words were punctuated by occasional tears and hopeful smiles that reflected her passionate feelings.

And Molly felt her own eyes fill as she realized that Abbey might finally find the happiness and contentment that had eluded her for so long.

The same happiness and contentment that had so recently slipped from her own grasp.

* * *

Harcourt Castle was everything Fiona had wanted for her wedding reception and the night was beautiful—if a little anticlimactic after the celebration at the royal palace in Tesoro del Mar. There were twinkling lights and soft music and waiters dressed in black tie circulating with trays of hot hors d'oeuvres and cold champagne. In the arbor where Fiona and Scott had originally intended to exchange their vows, a screen had been set up so that the guests could watch the video of the ceremony that was performed in Tesoro del Mar.

"It was a truly beautiful ceremony," Theresa said, dabbing her eyes.

"You could have been there," Molly reminded her, to which her grandmother shook her head firmly.

"If God wanted me to fly, he would have given me wings," she said, as she had so many times before.

"He didn't give you wheels, either, but that never stopped you from driving," her husband noted.

It was the only real issue on which Molly had ever heard her grandparents disagree—because Lawrence longed to travel and see the world and Theresa didn't.

"But what was with those vows?" Lawrence asked now. "I never heard anything like that before."

"We wrote our own," Fiona explained.

"What for?" her grandfather demanded. "Something wrong with the usual ones?"

"Times change," Theresa reminded him.

"You're telling me," Lawrence grumbled. "They don't even ask a wife to 'obey' anymore. When we got married, you promised to 'obey'."

"And how long did that last?" Scott asked.

"We've been married sixty-four years," Lawrence told his

newest grandson-in-law. "Because Theresa knows who's the boss."

"I certainly do, dear," his wife agreed, and took his arm to lead him away from the circle of their grandchildren.

"I think we all know who's the boss in that marriage," Jason said.

"Grandma definitely makes the decisions," Abbey said, linking her arm through her husband's. "But she manages to do it in a way that lets Grandpa thinks he's making them."

"Everyone needs some illusions," Scott said.

"And what are yours?" his bride wanted to know.

"Well, everyone but me," he said, wrapping his arms around his wife. "Because I have everything I could ever want right here."

Molly looked away when Scott bent his head to kiss Fiona—and found Eric looking at her.

"Cold?" Eric asked, slipping an arm across her shoulders when she shivered in response to the breeze that blew through the open windows.

She shook her head, because she wasn't anymore. And she was no longer surprised at how attuned he was to her needs, or by his willingness to meet them.

In the distance, Molly saw her grandfather hand a glass of champagne to his wife and brushed his lips against hers, and she knew that her grandparents were proof positive that love could and did last.

Looking around, she noticed that almost everyone was paired up with someone else, and as she stood there in the warmth and comfort of Eric's arms, she wondered if maybe she'd been too hasty in turning her back on the possibility of her own "happily ever after."

Eric thought something had shifted in his relationship with Molly that night, but two days later, on the day that they were scheduled to return to Tesoro del Mar, he wondered if he'd only imagined it. Once again he'd woken up to have breakfast with her grandparents, and once again Molly was already gone.

He knew where she was this time—she'd gone to the restaurant to sign the final papers to turn management of Shea's over to her sister and brother-in-law. He didn't think it had been an easy decision for her to make but, aside from telling him of the decision, she hadn't discussed it with him.

"You seem a little preoccupied this morning," Theresa said to Eric.

"I guess I'm just thinking of everything I'll have to do when I get back tonight," he told her.

"You're anxious to get back, aren't you?"

"I've enjoyed the time we've spent here," he said. "But there are business matters that need to be attended to."

"Can I tell you a story?" Theresa asked, in what seemed to him an abrupt change of topic.

"Okay," he agreed cautiously.

"It happened a long time ago—I can't remember exactly how long ago, although I do remember that Lawrence and I had only been married a few years because we were still living in that little bungalow on Chetwood Street. It wasn't much of a house, but there were some beautiful big trees in the backyard that would be filled with birds every summer.

"Anyway, I was outside one morning, weeding the garden. We used to grow our own vegetables back then, too, and it was my job to tend to them because Lawrence was working almost round-the-clock at the diner. That's all that Shea's was at the time—a twelve-by-twelve diner that served simple meals to simple folks."

She carried the coffeepot to the table and refilled his cup, and Eric settled in to listen. He wasn't yet sure what the point of this story was—or even if Theresa had one—but over the past couple of days, he'd spent a lot of time with Molly's grandmother and found that he genuinely enjoyed her company.

And whatever the topic of conversation, she inevitably had a story. Or she made one up. He was never quite sure whether her tales were fact or fiction, but she spun them so well it didn't really matter. He figured it was a talent she'd passed on to her granddaughter, as Molly had finally let him see some of the children's stories she'd been writing and told him that Lara had put her in touch with an editor who wanted to take a look at them. He'd been thrilled for her and proud of her, and quite impressed when he'd been given the chance to read what she'd written.

"Are you paying attention to this?" Theresa demanded, her eyes narrowed on him.

"Of course," he said. "You were outside weeding the garden."

"Yes, wrestling with some nasty pricklepoppy that was trying to strangle the roots of my tomato plants," she continued. "And right there in the dirt, I found a baby bird that had fallen out of its nest—or maybe been knocked out by a bigger bird. 'Cause this one was a tiny thing, and helpless. It might have been a sparrow, though I don't remember for sure. I didn't really know what to do with it, but I knew it would die if I just left it there, so I carried it inside. I kept it fed and gave it a little bed to sleep in while its injuries healed.

"Lawrence made me a little cage for it, so that it wouldn't try to fly too soon and hurt itself again. But by the time it was healed and ready to fly, I didn't want to let it go. It started to fight against the cage, demanding to be let free, and then one day it just suddenly stopped fighting, as if it recognized the futility of beating its wings against the walls that held it. And then it stopped singing, too.

"So I took the cage outside and finally released it. I watched it fly farther and farther away until I couldn't see it anymore because of the tears in my eyes.

"It was about a week later—I was in the garden again—when it came back. I wasn't sure it was the same bird at first, until it perched right on the fence where I was working and chirped at me. And I realized then how wrong I'd been to keep that bird inside a cage, to make it stay with me. That it would only ever be able to sing if it was free."

He picked up his cup, surprised to find it empty again. He'd been so caught up in the story he hadn't realized he'd drank it, but not so caught up that he didn't see the point she was trying to make.

"You think Molly feels trapped," he guessed.

"I think she feels that the circumstances have limited her options."

He frowned. "Three days ago, you gave me the impression that you wanted me to marry your granddaughter."

"*I* do want you to marry my granddaughter," she said. "But over the past couple of days, I've finally accepted that might not be what Molly wants."

"Are you suggesting now that I should just give up? That I should let her go?"

"I'm saying that she'll always resent feeling as if she had no choice."

He could understand that, but just the thought of being without Molly left his heart feeling as empty and hollow as he knew his life would be without her.

"I love her," he said, suddenly realizing it was true.

"I know you do," she said, and patted his arm, obviously not as surprised by the revelation as he was. "And that's why I know you'll do the right thing."

"What if I let her go and she doesn't come back?"

"Then it wasn't meant to be," she said simply.

He shook his head. He wouldn't—couldn't—believe that. Nothing in his life had ever seemed as right as being with Molly.

And yet, he knew her grandmother had a point.

You made me think that I had a choice, but I never really did.

If he took Molly back to Tesoro del Mar with him now, he would always wonder if she'd gone because she wanted to be with him or because she felt she had no other options.

He had to open the door and let her fly.

Chapter Fourteen

Molly spent the morning at Shea's finalizing the details of the agreement that would transfer ownership of the restaurant to Abbey and Jason. Though it was difficult to let go of the business that had been her life for so many years, she knew it was time. The restaurant had once seemed so inextricably linked to her father, but now Molly understood that Shea's was just a building on a piece of property. It was the memories that were the true legacy, and she would take those memories with her wherever she went.

And right now, her plan was to start a new life in Tesoro del Mar. Regardless of what arrangement she came to with Eric about their baby, she wanted her daughter to be close to her father and she knew that could only happen if she was living in Tesoro del Mar. It wasn't hard to imagine a life in a country she'd already fallen in love with—it *was* hard to imagine a life without the man she loved.

Maybe you need to consider that marrying him isn't a completely unreasonable idea.

She sighed as her grandmother's words echoed in the back of her mind.

Was it unreasonable to want the man she loved to love her back?

But even if, by some miracle, he did fall in love with her—would love be enough to make a marriage work?

She knew there were no guarantees in life—except that she was guaranteed to live her life alone if she didn't stop hiding behind her fears and go after what she really wanted.

And what she really wanted was Eric.

With her heart lighter than it had been in days, Molly didn't worry about the fact that the rental car wasn't in the driveway when she got back to her grandparents' house. In fact, she didn't think anything of it until she went up to her room and saw the envelope on the dresser with her name on it.

Frowning, she tore open the flap.

Dear Molly,

By the time you find this note, you're probably wondering where I am and why I'm not hovering over you to make sure your bags are packed so we can head back to Tesoro del Mar.

I've made a lot of mistakes in my life, but none that I regret more than the mistakes I've made from the very beginning in my relationship with you. I don't mean our baby—though our child might have been unplanned, I have never regretted her existence. But I do regret everything that's happened since I found out you were pregnant and every attempt I made to manipulate or coerce you into doing things my way. Parenting should be a joint venture. Marriage should be a true partnership.

Anton has filed a flight plan and we are scheduled to leave at four o'clock. I figured this would give you enough time after you got back from your meeting at the restaurant to pack and get to the airport if you want to come back to Tesoro del Mar with me.

If you're surprised that I'm giving you a choice, you might be even more surprised to know why—because I love you, Molly.

It seems strange to say those words for the first time on paper, but I couldn't leave without letting you know how I feel. It's not just the first time I've expressed those words to you, but the first time ever. I've never felt about another woman the way I feel about you. Before you came into my life I was lost, drifting. You changed everything for me.

I hope you know that I would do anything for you, give you anything you wanted if it was within my power to do so. And if all you want is your freedom, I will let you go.

As I write this note, I'm hoping with everything in my heart that you will be on the plane with me when it goes back to Tesoro del Mar tonight. But I want you to know that whatever you decide, I will love you always.

Eric

Molly raced down the stairs, Eric's letter clenched in her fist. She found her grandmother in the kitchen, humming to herself as she dropped spoonfuls of batter onto a tray. Her grandfather was at the table, drinking a cup of coffee and munching on warm oatmeal-raisin cookies.

The scene was homey and normal—a snapshot of the life she'd claimed she wanted, and a picture that was completely wrong without Eric in it.

Her grandmother looked up, smiled at her. "Want some cookies, honey?"

"Fresh pot of coffee, too," her grandfather said. "Decaf."

She shook her head. "No, thanks. Did you know Eric was gone?"

"Of course." Theresa slid the tray into the oven.

"He came into the garage to say goodbye, and to thank us for our hospitality." Lawrence chuckled. "And he said it with a straight face, even after four nights on that awful sofa bed."

Molly sank into a chair across from her grandfather. "And then he just left?"

Theresa's brow furrowed. "You didn't know he was going back today?"

"I didn't know he was going back *without me.*"

"I would think you'd be relieved," her grandmother said. "You were the one who told me how incompatible you are."

Molly sighed. "You told him the bird story, didn't you?"

Theresa sniffed. "It's a good story."

"What bird story?" Lawrence asked, reaching for another cookie.

Molly shook her head. "The same story that she told me after my fiancé came home from Vegas married to my sister."

"Actually, it wasn't quite the same," Theresa said. "Having the bird come back with a mate this time would have completely changed the message."

"I love you, Grandma, but you've got to let me live my life."

"That's just what I told Eric," her grandmother said. "And living your life means accepting responsibility for your own choices. You can choose to stay or you can choose to go, but now there will be no doubt that the choice is yours."

Molly looked at her grandfather. "Has she always been this sneaky?"

"One of the reasons I married her," he agreed. "I wanted to be sure she'd always be on my side."

"So what's it going to be?" Theresa asked her granddaughter.

Molly stood up. "I'm going to fly."

* * *

There were charter flights to Tesoro del Mar twice a week.

Eric knew that and tried to take comfort in the fact that if Molly wasn't at the airport by the time Anton was ready to go, it would be easy enough for her to take another plane to the island. Assuming, of course, that she wanted to come back. And right now, with no sign of Molly anywhere, he knew that was a big assumption.

"I'm going to do the final flight check," Anton said.

But it was more a question than a statement, and Eric knew he was seeking confirmation that Eric intended to stick with their schedule.

The pilot had been surprised when the prince arrived without Molly and asked if she'd been delayed. Eric had told him, honestly, that he wasn't certain if Molly would be flying with them. Anton had never been one to question his boss and he didn't do so now, but Eric knew he was puzzled by the response.

"Go ahead," he said now.

The pilot nodded and ducked outside.

He would walk around the outside, visually confirming that everything was as it should be, then double-check all the gauges and instruments that had already been double-checked. Anton was nothing if not meticulous about the care and operation of his plane.

While he was waiting, Eric opened his laptop and checked his e-mail. He'd had a brief meeting with Scott while he was in town, updating his friend on the progress of DELconnex International. He knew he wouldn't be able to focus on work, but if he was staring at the computer screen, he wouldn't be staring out the window watching for Molly.

He read a few e-mails—and read them again when he realized he hadn't comprehended a single word the first time through.

When he heard footsteps on the metal stairs, he closed the lid and pushed the computer aside.

But when he looked up, it wasn't Anton in the doorway—it was Molly.

Her smile was soft, her eyes warm and glowing with the familiar light he loved.

"Is this plane going to Tesoro del Mar?" she asked.

He stood up, wanting nothing so much as he wanted to haul her into his arms and hold on to her, to know for sure that she was there, that she was real. But the choice needed to be hers, so he stayed where he was standing and said, "It can go wherever you want to go."

"I want to go home," she said, and breached the distance between them.

Then she was in his arms and he was holding her as close as their baby would allow. And she was holding him, too.

"It's almost four o'clock," he murmured the words into her hair.

She tilted her head back. "Have you been waiting long?"

"I feel as if I've been waiting for you my whole life," he said, tightening his arms around her.

"I was going to make you wait longer," she admitted. "I was going to wait in the hangar until Anton started the engines, but I thought that might be cutting it too close."

"You wanted me to suffer," he guessed.

"I figured it was only fair considering that I've been suffering for months knowing that I was falling in love with you and believing you could never feel the same way."

"It turns out you were wrong," he said.

"I was wrong about something else," she admitted. "I thought I needed you—at least for the sake of our baby—and I resented you for that. But when we came back to Texas, I realized that I could make a life for her on my own if it was what I wanted.

Maybe I couldn't give her the kind of life you could, but it would be a good one.

"But the more I thought about that, the more I realized that while I *could* do it, it wasn't what I wanted to do. I want to raise our child together. I want to spend my life with you."

"Your wish—" he brushed his lips against hers "—is my command."

After the debacle at the airport, Molly wasn't surprised to return to Tesoro del Mar to find that the news of her pregnancy had made headlines in all the local papers. Another Royal Baby in the New Year? Prince Eric a Daddy? And, her least favorite, Heir Apparent, above a photo of her in profile with the baby bulge clearly visible.

In response to all the furor, Eric decided to hold a press conference with Molly by his side, confirming that they were expecting a child early in the new year. It was their first official public appearance together, and though Molly had worried about having so much attention focused on her, she was glad that she and Eric would no longer have to hide their relationship or her pregnancy.

It was on their way back home after the press conference that Molly said, "I want to get married on Christmas Eve."

Eric shifted so that he was facing her. "Do you mean in general, if you ever get married?" he asked. "Or do you mean that you want to marry me?"

"I want to marry you."

"*This* Christmas Eve?"

She nodded, grinning. "Think we can pull off a royal wedding in two months?"

"We can do anything if it means putting my ring on your finger," he said, and sealed the promise with a long, slow kiss.

Molly melted against him, her heart sighing with contentment even as her body started to stir again with longing.

"Why Christmas Eve?" he asked later.

"Because Christmas hasn't been a happy occasion for me in a very long time," she admitted, "and I want to change that."

"What happened?"

She swallowed around the tightness in her throat. "My dad died on Christmas Eve. It will be ten years ago this year."

He tucked her closer to him. "I can see how that would put a damper on the holidays."

She nodded.

"Christmas Eve mass is a huge celebration here," he told her. "And it would be a perfect opportunity to introduce you as my wife to the people of Tesoro del Mar."

"You do realize I'm going to be hugely pregnant by Christmas Eve, don't you?"

He rubbed his hand over the curve of her belly. "You mean, you're not hugely pregnant now?"

She swatted him playfully. "Just remember, that's your baby that has me so bent out of shape."

"Our baby," he said, and dipped his head to kiss her lips, then her belly, then her lips again. "Another good thing about getting married on Christmas Eve is it would be convenient for your family to stay and spend the holidays with us."

She was touched that he wanted to include them, but she shook her head. "As much as I'd love to have my family here, I don't think that's a likely scenario. My grandmother refuses to even go near an airport, never mind set foot on an airplane. Abbey and Jason are finally getting their marriage back on track and are busy with the restaurant, and Fiona and Scott are just settling into their lives as newlyweds."

"Would it be easier, then, if we got married in Texas?"

"I'm going to be thirty-eight weeks along by Christmas Eve," she reminded him. "I can't imagine any doctor giving approval for me to fly so close to the end of my pregnancy."

"We could go back now, stay there for the wedding and after, until the baby's born."

She stared at him, stunned that he would even make such a suggestion. "You'd be willing to do that?"

"I love you," he said simply.

And she knew then, without a doubt, that it was true.

She kissed him softly, appreciatively. "Thank you for even considering it," she said. "But I want to be married, have our baby and start our life together right here."

Now that the date had been set, Molly was busy overseeing preparations for the big day. They'd decided to have the ceremony in the main parlor, which—along with the rest of the house—was being transformed by the small army that Carla had hired expressly for that purpose. While the holiday decorating was a project she would usually have tackled herself, the housekeeper insisted that everything had to be on a much grander scale this year because they weren't just preparing for the celebrations of the season but for the next royal wedding.

When the work was finished, it seemed that there wasn't a doorway in the entire house that wasn't draped with evergreen boughs and velvet ribbons or a table that wasn't adorned with a pot of holiday flowers or a vase of pretty glass balls. As Eric and Molly walked through the house, she was both awed and amazed by the attention to detail and couldn't think of a single thing she would change—until they got to the front parlor and she saw the towering but sadly barren tree beside the fireplace.

"Decorating the Christmas tree was one of our family traditions," Eric explained. "Every year, it was something my father, my mother and my brothers and I did together. I'd like to continue that tradition for our family."

Molly had been feeling twinges in her lower back as they walked through the house, but she didn't tell Eric because she knew he would insist that she rest, and she really wanted to share in this tradition with him. So they decorated the tree together, stringing up what seemed like thousands of tiny lights, unwinding miles of thick gold ribbon, hanging hundreds of shiny red and gold balls.

When the last ornament had finally been hung, Molly stood back in the circle of Eric's arms to admire their efforts.

"It looks pretty good for our first Christmas tree, doesn't it?" he said.

Our first Christmas. The words were a promise of years to come, of their future together, and they brought tears to her eyes. "It looks great," she agreed. "But there's still something missing."

"The tree topper," he suddenly remembered, and gestured to a large box on the table—a box she knew hadn't been there a moment before.

She opened the lid to reveal an exquisite angel with a delicately sculpted porcelain face and arms, in a flowing gown of elegant ecru lace over cream-colored satin. The wings were iridescent and shot through with gold threads. There was a gold ribbon around her waist, and at the end of the ribbon—

Her breath caught in her throat.

Eric smiled. "I know we've taken a lot of steps out of order in our relationship," he said. "But I thought we should be formally engaged before we got married."

"It's...wow."

He smiled and steered her over to the sofa, gently nudging her to sit. She sank onto the soft edge, her knees trembling, her heart pounding so hard the discomfort in her back was momentarily forgotten.

She didn't know why she was so nervous—they'd already set the date for the wedding and plans were well underway. But the thoughtfulness and romance of the moment seemed to have knocked her off her feet—and that was before Eric got down on one knee beside her.

He untied the ribbon, freeing the circle of gold and diamonds to drop into his palm.

"It's not a traditional engagement ring," he admitted. "In fact, it wasn't originally an engagement ring at all, but an eternity band that my father gave to my mother for their twenty-fifth wedding anniversary. When my mother died, it came to me.

"The circle of diamonds is said to represent unending love," he explained, taking her left hand in his. "As I will love you, Molly. Forever and always."

Chapter Fifteen

Eric slid the ring onto Molly's finger and linked their hands together. She squeezed his. Hard. He noticed her other hand had gone to her stomach and her face had gone pale.

"What's wrong?" he asked.

"I'm not sure. I've been having these twinges in my lower back for a few hours that I didn't think were anything, but now..."

"Now what?"

"I think I've been having...contractions."

"But—" He didn't know what to say. It was as if everything inside of him, including his brain, had gone numb with shock. "But you're not due until the new year."

"I'm aware of that," she said, a little breathlessly.

"And first babies are more commonly late than early," he added.

"Yeah, well, tell that to your daughter."

"Lara went early with William," he noted. "But only a few

days, and he wasn't her first. Matthew didn't come until four days after the due date."

"Eric!"

He shook his head, and turned his attention back to the woman who was going to have his baby—maybe a lot sooner than either of them had anticipated.

"Do you think you could…call the…doctor?"

Eric raced to the phone.

Dr. Marotta asked about the frequency and duration of Molly's contractions, whether her water had broken, if she was having back pain, spotting or bleeding. Eric's answers were "every fifteen to twenty minutes," "about sixty seconds," "no," "yes" and "thank God, no." To which the doctor advised that there was probably nothing to get excited about just yet, but he would come over to check the mom-to-be, anyway.

"The baby's not due for another three weeks," Eric said when the doctor had finished his exam.

Dr. Marotta's eyes sparkled with humor. "Babies come when they're ready not when their fathers are, Your Highness."

"Should she go to the hospital?"

The doctor looked at Molly. "Have you changed your mind about wanting to have the baby at home?"

"No," Molly told him. "Not if there's no risk to the baby."

"At this point, there's nothing to suggest either you or the baby are in any danger," Dr. Marotta assured her.

Which wasn't the unconditional guarantee Eric had hoped for.

The doctor left them with his cell-phone number and instructions to call when her contractions were coming about five minutes apart, or sooner if they had any questions.

When the door had closed behind the departing doctor, Molly squeezed Eric's hand. "I'm sorry."

"Why are you sorry?"

"Because I know it was important to you for us to be married before she was born."

"What's important," he said, "is that she's born healthy."

"Dr. Marotta doesn't seem worried that she's coming early, does he?"

His only response was a quick shake of his head and a terse, "No."

"Then you shouldn't be, either," she told him, and he realized she hadn't been seeking reassurance, but to reassure.

"I know," he said, then admitted, "I'd just feel better if you were in the hospital where they have all the high-tech equipment and the fancy drugs."

She managed to smile because she knew he was genuinely concerned. She'd had a few moments herself in which she'd second-guessed the decision to have their baby in the house where she and Eric had been living for the past six months—the house where he and his brothers had been born. But as her due date grew nearer, she grew more settled in her conviction that it was the right thing to do. She didn't have a lot to give to her baby in the way of family history so she felt it was important to help carry on whatever traditions she could.

She squeezed Eric's hand again, but this time it was an involuntary response to the contraction that tightened her womb. The contractions weren't so painful—not yet, anyway—but they were irregular, and it was the unexpectedness that always jarred her.

"Are you sure you don't want drugs?" Eric asked.

"Right now I'm not sure of anything," she admitted. "Except that I'm really glad you're here with me."

"As if I'd be anywhere else."

They took a long walk around the grounds together while Carla bustled around nervously and Stefan prepared a light snack for the mother-to-be. Then they decided to follow the doctor's advice and get some rest, because he'd warned that rest wouldn't be an option when the contractions increased in frequency and intensity.

Molly did manage to nap briefly, and when she woke, she found her back snuggled tightly against Eric's front, his hand splayed over the curve of her belly and the rigid shaft of his arousal pressing against her buttocks.

"I'm guessing that you're not sleeping," she said dryly.

He chuckled softly. "I was resting—until you started squirming around."

"I apologize."

"Please don't."

She smiled, then sucked in a breath as a contraction hit.

Eric's hand moved in gentle, soothing circles over her belly. "You managed to sleep through a couple of mild ones," he said. "And they're still about fifteen minutes apart."

She put her hand over his, linking their fingers together. "I just want so much for her to be born."

"We've done everything we can to speed things along. Now we just have to be patient."

"We haven't quite done everything," she noted, deliberately wriggling against him.

"Molly," he warned.

She rolled over—not an easy task considering her current size and condition—so that she was facing him. "Don't you remember what that book said about sexual activity helping to bring on labor?"

"Yeah." He swallowed. "I remember."

"Lara told me it worked for her when she was pregnant with Matthew."

He winced. "Please. I love my sister-in-law, but I don't want to think about her and my brother…you know."

"Then you probably don't want to know that Jewel also advocated its success."

"No—in fact, I think now would be a good time for you to stop talking," he said.

She closed her mouth.

Then she reached down between their bodies and pressed her hand to the front of his pants, stroking him through the fabric.

He groaned. "You're killing me here."

"I promise you—" she nibbled on his lip, tasting, teasing "—that isn't my intention."

"What do you think Dr. Marotta would say if he walked in here right now?"

She scraped her teeth over his jaw. "He'd probably say that you should have locked the door."

"I'm not convinced he would approve of this."

"He was the one who made a point of saying that he'd be gone a couple of hours."

She kissed him again, slowly, deeply, using her tongue and teeth on his mouth while her hands got busy with his belt. Then she reached inside and—

He rolled off of the mattress.

She wasn't sure whether to be insulted or amused by how quickly he moved away from her. "Where are you going?"

His only response was to flip the lock on the door, and her heart rate kicked up a notch.

Molly smiled as he came back to the bed. His pace was a little more leisurely now, his movements deliberate, the heat in his eyes scorching.

She'd thought her sex drive would decrease as the size of the baby increased, but found that the opposite seemed to be true. Both of Eric's sisters-in-law had assured her that wasn't unusual, though Molly couldn't remember how the topic had come up in conversation or why it had been so easy for her to talk about such intimate topics with the women who were married to Eric's brothers.

The mattress dipped as Eric lowered himself onto it, and when he brushed his lips against hers, all other thoughts fled her mind.

"We've probably got about an hour left," he told her.

"An hour," she echoed on a sigh as his hands skimmed down her sides to the hem of her nightshirt, then below.

She sucked in a breath at the rush of air that cooled her heated flesh when he yanked the garment up and over her head, then giggled when he unceremoniously tossed it aside and pounced on her. "You don't seem so uncertain now."

"I realized this will probably be my last chance to get naked with you for the next couple of months, and I certainly wasn't going to let that opportunity go."

But despite the teasing words, it wasn't his own gratification he seemed concerned with, but hers. He kissed her, slowly and deeply, exploring her mouth with his lips and teeth and tongue. She'd never known a man who derived so much pleasure from just kissing—and still gave so much more.

And while he was kissing her, he was touching her. His hands skimmed over her body, from her shoulders to her elbows to her wrists. From her hips to her belly to her breasts. Gentle strokes, featherlight touches and tantalizing caresses.

He let her guide him, using her soft sighs and murmurs to direct every pass of his hands and touch of his lips. He was so incredibly focused, so selflessly giving, that she forgot this was supposed to be about hurrying her labor along as she lost herself in the pleasure he was giving her.

His palms grazed over the tight buds of her nipples, a light touch that nevertheless shot rockets of sensation through her body. She gasped, then moaned when his hands closed over her breasts, squeezing gently.

Then he dipped his head, and his mouth—that wonderfully talented mouth—closed around one peaked nipple and he suckled.

She felt her womb tighten and tense with pain, but there was pleasure, too, as he continued to use his lips and tongue on her.

She felt the rush of liquid between her thighs as the spasms continued to wrack her body and her fingers dug into his shoulders as she held on through the waves that lifted her up and up.

Molly's labor started in earnest after that. As Dr. Marotta had warned, there was no opportunity to rest or relax when her contractions stretched to two minutes and weren't coming much further apart than that.

Through it all, Molly never once cried out in pain or screamed at him. She remained quietly and intently focused, she kept her breathing regular and steady without needing to be coached to do so and she kept her gaze focused on the vase of fresh flowers on the other side of the room, which Carla had brought in as a focal point. In fact, Molly was doing such a good job managing her own labor that Eric was beginning to feel extraneous.

He knew she wasn't deliberately shutting him out. She was just trying to handle giving birth as she'd handled everything else in her life since her father had died and her former fiancé had abandoned her—on her own.

Her grandmother had said that Molly was too stubborn for her own good, but Eric understood that she didn't like to depend on anyone else because there had never really been anyone she could depend on. He was determined to prove to her that he was that someone.

So while she never asked for his help, he stayed by her side. He offered her ice chips, he wiped her face and throat with a cool cloth. And he noticed that she eventually shifted her focus from the flowers to him.

Then, when the doctor's examination confirmed that she was fully dilated and ready to start pushing, she reached for his hand and linked their fingers together. "Stay with me?"

"Always," he promised her, and meant it.

And he was right there to hear the first cries when their baby was born twenty-two minutes later.

It didn't take long for Molly and Eric and Princess Margaret Theresa Santiago to settle into a routine. The routine basically being that the princess cried and both of her parents jumped, which meant that the baby was always fed and dry and being cuddled in one pair of arms or another, and her mother and father were exhausted.

By day four, Molly was ready to suggest a postponement of their wedding, certain she would end up sleepwalking down the aisle. It was a testament to his own state of fatigue that Eric actually considered it.

It was Carla who put her foot down—she'd been working her tail off to make sure everything was ready for the royal wedding and, dammit, there was going to be a royal wedding. The day before Christmas Eve, she called in reinforcements—bringing in Lara and Jewel to take turns with the baby so her exhausted parents could sleep.

So it was that Molly awoke on Christmas Eve morning feeling rested—and with enough energy to be excited about finally becoming Eric's wife. When Maggie started to demand her breakfast, Molly tucked her against her breast as Eric wandered out of the bathroom, fully dressed.

"What are you doing up so early?"

"I've got to get to the airport to pick up your Christmas gift."

"My Christmas gift is at the airport?"

He glanced at his watch. "They will be in about an hour."

Her breath caught. "They?"

He lowered himself onto the edge of the mattress and leaned over to kiss her softly. "My family's going to be here for our wedding. I thought that yours should be, too."

"But we talked about this—"

"And you didn't think I could get your grandmother on an airplane," he remembered.

"She's coming?"

"Both your grandparents and Fiona and Scott." He shrugged. "One of the perks of having access to a private plane."

"You think my grandmother actually got on it?"

"I know she did. It's not one of those questionable commercial aircraft, you know," he said, no doubt an exact quote of Theresa's words. "And she figured if the Santiago jet was good enough for the royal family of Tesoro del Mar, it was good enough for her."

She smiled through her tears. "This is, without a doubt, the best Christmas present ever."

He shook his head. "It doesn't even compare to what you gave me."

She stroked a finger gently over the baby's cheek. "She is pretty incredible, isn't she?"

"She is," he agreed. "But I didn't just mean our daughter."

"Well, your other presents are wrapped and under the tree, and you're not getting them until tomorrow."

He put his arms around her, so their baby was snuggled between them. "I was referring to hope and happiness and dreams for our future together."

She tipped her head back. "I gave you all that?"

"You changed my life," he told her. "The day I saw that neon sign as I drove around the curve in the highway."

"Jason wants to get rid of the neon," she told him. "It doesn't fit with the image they want for the restaurant."

"We'll have the sign shipped over here and hang it above the bed," he said. And though she smiled again, he had to ask, "Are you okay with the changes they're making?"

"It's their restaurant now," she said simply.

"Do you miss it?"

She shook her head. "How could I when I have you and Maggie, and now a contract to write children's books?" The offer had come through less than a week earlier, and Molly had been so stunned when the editor had told her why he was calling that she'd dropped the phone, inadvertently hanging up on him. Thankfully, he'd called right back.

"Your grandmother is so tickled about that."

"She always said I was a writer."

"She was right." He snuggled her close. "You haven't asked why Abbey and Jason aren't here."

"This would be difficult for my sister," Molly said. "I understand."

He shook his head. "She wanted to be here—she was very excited about meeting her niece and, up until two days ago, she and Jason planned to make the trip, too."

"What happened?"

"Family Services called, asking if they could take in a seven-month-old boy. They know it might only be a temporary placement," he said, "but they couldn't turn him down."

Molly nodded, her throat tight. "I think it's going to be a really good Christmas for Abbey and Jason this year, too."

"Speaking of Christmas," Eric said, lifting the now-sleeping baby from her arms, "it's going to be just that in less than twenty-four hours, so if we want to be married before then, you'd better get up and start getting ready."

"I want to be married before then." Molly took the hand he offered and slid out of bed and into his arms. "I'm ready for my happily ever after to begin."

Epilogue

PRINCE CELEBRATES HOLIDAY WITH
WEDDING BELLS & BABY BOTTLES
by Alex Girard

The holiday season is a busy time, but this year it was even more so than usual for His Royal Highness Prince Eric Santiago. The former naval officer turned corporate exec celebrated Christmas Eve at Estado de las Morales, his family's ancestral estate on the northern coast, by exchanging vows with Molly Shea, a native of San Antonio whom he met while visiting a friend in Texas earlier this year.

The wedding was planned to precede the birth of the couple's first child, due early in the new year. The young princess, however, made her arrival three weeks early in order to be present at her parents' nuptials.

The intimate ceremony was witnessed by a small gathering of family and close friends. Afterward, the bride and groom attended Christmas Eve mass at the Cathedral to announce their marriage and present their daughter, Princess Margaret Theresa Santiago, to the people of Tesoro del Mar.

In response to the urging of the crowd, the prince pulled a sprig of mistletoe from his pocket and held it over his bride's head before giving her a kiss that was hot enough to warm even the coldest winter day, and sizzling enough to ensure that it was going to be a very happy Christmas for the newlyweds and their newly expanded family. Feliz Navidad!

* * * * *

One

Hunter Cabot, Navy SEAL, had a healing bullet wound in his side, thirty days' leave and, apparently, a wife he'd never met.

On the drive into his hometown of Springville, California, he stopped for gas at Charlie Evans's service station. That's where the trouble started.

"Hunter! Man, it's good to see you! Margie didn't tell us you were coming home."

"Margie?" Hunter leaned back against the front fender of his black pickup truck and winced as his side gave a small twinge of pain. Silently then, he watched as the man he'd known since high school filled his tank.

Charlie grinned, shook his head and pumped gas. "Guess your wife was lookin' for a little 'alone' time with you, huh?"

"My—" Hunter couldn't even say the word. *Wife?* He didn't have a wife. "Look, Charlie…"

"Don't blame her, of course," his friend said with a wink as he finished up and put the gas cap back on. "You being gone all the time with the SEALs must be hard on the ol' love life."

He'd never had any complaints, Hunter thought, frowning at the man still talking a mile a minute. "What're you—"

"Bet Margie's anxious to see you. She told us all about that R & R trip you two took to Bali." Charlie's dark brown eyebrows lifted and wiggled.

"Charlie…"

"Hey, it's okay, you don't have to say a thing, man."

What the hell could he say? Hunter shook his head, paid for his gas and as he left, told himself Charlie was just losing it. Maybe the guy had been smelling gas fumes too long.

But as it turned out, it wasn't just Charlie. Stopped at a red light on Main Street, Hunter glanced out his window to smile at Mrs. Harker, his second-grade teacher who was now at least a hundred years old. In the middle of the crosswalk, the old lady stopped and shouted, "Hunter Cabot, you've got yourself a wonderful wife. I hope you appreciate her."

Scowling now, he only nodded at the old woman—the only teacher who'd ever scared the crap out of him. What the hell was going on here? Was everyone but him nuts?

His temper beginning to boil, he put up with a few more comments about his "wife" on the drive through town before finally pulling into the wide, circular drive leading to the Cabot mansion. Hunter didn't have a clue what was going on, but he planned to get to the bottom of it. Fast.

He grabbed his duffel bag, stalked into the house and paid no attention to the housekeeper, who ran at him, fluttering both hands. "Mr. Hunter!"

"Sorry, Sophie," he called out over his shoulder as he took the stairs two at a time. "Need a shower, then we'll talk."

He marched down the long, carpeted hallway to the rooms that were always kept ready for him. In his suite, Hunter tossed the duffel down and stopped dead. The shower in his bathroom was running. His *wife?*

Anger and curiosity boiled in his gut, creating a churning mass that had him moving forward without even thinking about it. He opened the bathroom door to a wall of steam and the sound of a woman singing—off-key. Margie, no doubt.

Well, if she was his wife… Hunter walked across the room, yanked the shower door open and stared in at a curvy, naked, temptingly wet woman.

She whirled to face him, slapping her arms across her naked body while she gave a short, terrified scream.

Hunter smiled. "Hi, honey. I'm home."

* * * * *

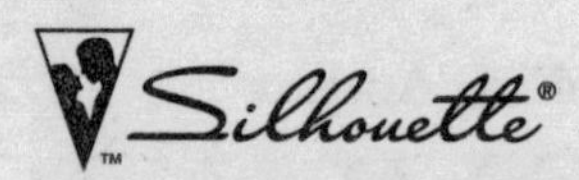

SPECIAL EDITION®

COMING NEXT MONTH

#1945 THE STRANGER AND TESSA JONES—Christine Rimmer
Bravo Family Ties
The Bravos meet the Jones Gang as two of Christine Rimmer's famous Special Edition families come together in one very special book. Snowed in with an amnesiac stranger during a freak blizzard, Tessa Jones soon finds out her guest is none other than heartbreaker Ash Bravo. And that's when things really heat up....

#1946 PLAIN JANE AND THE PLAYBOY—Marie Ferrarella
Fortunes of Texas: Return to Red Rock
To kill time at a New Year's party, playboy Jorge Mendoza shows the host's teenage son how to woo the ladies. The random target of Jorge's charms: wallflower Jane Gilliam. But with one kiss at midnight, introverted Jane turns the tables on this would-be Casanova, as the commitment-phobe falls for her hook, line and sinker!

#1947 COWBOY TO THE RESCUE—Stella Bagwell
Men of the West
Hired to investigate the mysterious death of the Sandbur Ranch matriarch's late husband, private investigator Christina Logan enlists the help of cowboy-to-the-core Lex Saddler, Sandbur's youngest—and singlest—scion. Together, they find the truth...and each other.

#1948 REINING IN THE RANCHER—Karen Templeton
Wed in the West
Horse breeder Johnny Griego is blindsided by the news—both his ex-girlfriend Thea Benedict *and* his teenage daughter are pregnant. Never one to shirk responsibility, Johnny does the right thing and proposes to Thea. But Thea wants happily-ever-after, not a mere marriage of convenience. Can she rein in the rancher enough to have both?

#1949 SINGLE MOM SEEKS...—Teresa Hill
All newly divorced Lily Tanner wants is a safe, happy life with her two adorable daughters. Until hunky FBI agent Nick Malone moves in next door with his orphaned nephew. Now the pretty single mom's single days just might be numbered....

#1950 I STILL DO—Christie Ridgway
During a chance reunion in Vegas, former childhood sweethearts Will Dailey and Emily Garner let loose a little and make good on an old pledge—to wed each other if they weren't otherwise taken by age thirty! But in the cold light of day, the firefighter and librarian's quickie marriage doesn't seem like such a bright idea. Would their whim last a lifetime?

SSECNM1208BPA